HECK'S GAMBLE

HECK & HOPE, BOOK 4

JOHN DEACON

Cover design by Angie on Fiverr

Edited by Karen Bennett

Want to know when my next book is released? SIGN UP HERE.

✻ Created with Vellum

PROLOGUE

Heck's Gamble is book four in the **Heck & Hope** series. I recommend reading the books in order, as they tell a continuing story. If you would like a refresher, here's the story so far, along with a list of characters.

Heck's Journey (Heck & Hope #1)

Orphaned at fourteen, Hector "Heck" Martin heads west, determined to see the far country and make a man of himself.

Along the way, he falls in love with bold and beautiful Hope Mullen. But Heck is too young and poor to marry, so he heads west again.

During a three-year journey, Heck crosses thousands of miles, becomes a bareknuckle boxer, a mountain man, and an

Indian fighter, and meets the likes of Kit Carson and Jim Bridger as he explores the gorgeous and deadly frontier.

Then, stopping by Fort Bent, he receives a letter that changes everything. Hope's family is daring the Oregon Trail.

Heck sets out to intercept and help them. Near the Oregon Trail in Wyoming, he throws in with another, younger orphan, Seeker, who becomes like a little brother to him.

Meanwhile, the Mullens face serious troubles—both outside and within the wagon train. When bandits attack, Mr. Mullen is badly injured, and the family loses its wagon and all their possessions. They are forced to live off the charity of the despicable Basil Paisley, a wealthy and cruel young man who wants to possess Hope.

Reunited with the Mullens, Heck saves them, kills Paisley and his thugs, and proposes to Hope, who happily accepts.

HECK'S VALLEY (HECK & HOPE #2)

As a mountain man and cavalry scout, Heck Martin handled every challenge on the Western frontier.

Now, however, he must care not only for himself but also his beloved Hope, her family, and his adopted brother, Seeker, in a remote wilderness populated by hostile Indians, bandits, and predators.

Most men would crumble under these circumstances, but Heck has enough love and courage to forge a new destiny in this mighty land. Filled with tough optimism and pioneering spirit, he vows to master the wilderness.

There is much to do.

Timber to cut. Cabins to build. Game to hunt. Land to plow and plant. A claim to stake. Caves to explore. A trading post to build. And hopefully, a happy wedding to share with the young woman he loves.

But Indians are moving through the land, and a gigantic grizzly is on the prowl. Meanwhile, 1850 brings record numbers of emigrants across the Oregon Trail. Not all are prepared, and as travel season comes to an end, a group of straggling emigrants limps into the valley, seeking sanctuary.

Heck and Hope agree to help, but not everyone should be trusted.

Most of the newcomers a good people. They bring important skills and work hard, helping mightily in the construction of the fort and the building of new roads.

Doctor Michael Skiff, who is also a pastor, marries Heck and Hope.

But newcomer Dave Chapman is secretly one of the bandits who attacked the Mullens' train and later got mostly wiped out by Heck and Seeker. He acts the part of a pleasant emigrant, but he really wants to kill Heck and steal away Hope and Amelia.

When Heck battles a giant grizzly bear, Dave shoots him in the back. Always tough, Heck barely manages to finish the bear and kill the backshooting bandit as well.

During Heck's long recovery, he comes to rely on his friends and family, who keep things moving. Eventually, he is able to return to the mysterious cave complex, where, in the final chapter, he discovers a massive nugget of gold.

· · ·

Heck's Gold (Heck & Hope #3)

After completing their fort, the residents of Heck's Valley brace for winter. Many speak of spring—and the possibility of staying here and working together to build a town in this breathtaking wilderness.

Heck and Hope don't know what the future holds, but so long as they are together, they face it with confidence.

But life on the frontier is never easy.

They have to guard their stock, keep the peace, and prepare defenses for spring, when the Sioux warriors who killed Seeker's parents will again come raiding.

When word of Heck's massive golden nugget leaks, there is trouble among the emigrants, but Heck handles it. He is determined to sit on the nugget indefinitely, as they don't need the money it represents.

After a brutal winter, most of the emigrants decide to stay. Working together, they create their town, which they dub Hope City.

With spring come raiders from the Bone Canyon Sioux. Seeker avenges his parents as the citizens of Hope City, with the help of Seeker's uncle, Black Cloud, ambush the raiders, wiping out all but one, a tough young brave named Little Bull, who rides back to his tribe carrying Heck's warning.

Jim Bridger shows up, bearing supplies and bad news. The price of the valley has gone up.

Accompanied by Bridger, Two Bits, and assayer Sam Collins, Heck travels to San Francisco and sell the nugget. Here, he gets involved with rough characters, including gang boss Bill

Getty and the new bareknuckle boxing champion of the West, Big Jess Heller.

Dodging Getty, Heck wagers everything on a fight against Heller. Beating the giant and reclaiming his old boxing title, Heck is suddenly flush with cash. He trades the nugget with Cattleman *Don* Vasquez for a herd of longhorn cattle, thereby making a mortal enemy in the nugget's would-be buyer, the richest man in California, gold baron Percival Dumay, who vows to get even with Heck.

On the trip home, Heck is attacked by Getty and his man but kills them easily.

Returning to the valley, he is overjoyed to be reunited with Hope—and to meet his newborn son, Hector Martin III, known as "Tor."

HECK'S GAMBLE (HECK & HOPE #4) PICKS UP A YEAR AFTER THE events of *Heck's Gold*, when prospectors are trickling into the region.

CAST OF CHARACTERS:

HECTOR "HECK" MARTIN, 17, KENTUCKY-BORN MOUNTAIN MAN with big frontier spirit, former bareknuckle boxing champion of the West, tall lean and powerful with a black hair and blue eyes, tough yet compassionate.

. . .

HOPE MULLEN, 17, HECK'S WIFE, KIND, IMPULSIVE, PLAYFUL, God-fearing, great with animals, a gifted nurse with auburn hair and green eyes.

SEEKER YATES, 12, HECK'S ADOPTED BROTHER, A HALF-Shoshone orphan wise in the ways of the wilderness who had been wary and lonesome until he met Heck.

MR. MULLEN: HOPE'S FATHER, A FORMER BOXER, TOUGH YET quick to laugh, recently recovered from severe wounds sustained on the Oregon Trail, loves his family fiercely.

MRS. MULLEN: HOPE'S MOTHER, INTELLIGENT AND LOVING, sober-minded, follower of Jesus and often the voice of wisdom.

TOM MULLEN: HOPE'S BROTHER, 19, A GIFTED LEATHERWORKER, smitten with Amelia Haines.

AMOS JOHNSON: A FRONTIER BARD SAVED BY HECK AND HOPE after a grizzly attack, travels the West chronicling the deeds of great men. After a long stay, he left Heck's Valley, headed for California and new stories.

. . .

BLACK CLOUD: SEEKER'S SHOSHONE UNCLE, WHO HELPED AVENGE the murder of his sister, Seeker's mother, by Sioux raiders.

JIM BRIDGER: THE FAMOUS MOUNTAIN MAN, HECK'S FRIEND.

TWO BITS: JIM BRIDGER'S SHOSHONE EMPLOYEE, WHO "WILL DO anything for two bits."

ABLE DEAN: HECK'S LAWYER.

LITTLE BULL: A STRONG YOUNG SIOUX WARRIOR WHO VOWS TO kill Heck and Seeker.

DON VASQUEZ: THE CATTLEMAN WHO BOUGHT HECK'S NUGGET for a herd of longhorns, some top cattle horses, and the service of vaqueros.

PERCIVAL DUMAY: A GOLD BARON, THE WEALTHIEST MAN IN California, angered over losing Heck's nugget, he is determined to settle the score.

MAJOR AVERY SCOTTSDALE: HECK'S OLD FRIEND FROM FORT Bent, now stationed at Fort Laramie.

. . .

THE EMIGRANTS

DOCTOR MICHAEL "DOC" SKIFF: BROAD-SHOULDERED AND bespectacled, Heck's best friend among the emigrants, a man of many talents, physician, pastor, fisherman, cook.

TITUS HAINES: WIDOWER, FORMER WAGON MASTER, schoolmaster, and cavalry officer.

AMELIA HAINES, 19, TITUS'S DAUGHTER AND TEACHING assistant, likes Tom Mullen, remarkably beautiful with dark hair and brown eyes, still reeling from the death of her mother.

SUSAN HAINES, 12, AMELIA'S SISTER.

SAM COLLINS: ASSAYER, HELPFUL.

TRACE BOON: YOUNG MINER, BROKE INTO HECK'S CABIN, LEFT Heck's Valley to join the California gold rush.

. . .

JEM PULCHER: TRACE BOON'S COUSIN, ALSO BROKE INTO HECK'S cabin and left for San Francisco.

MYLES MASON: FURNITURE MAKER, UNDERTAKER.

RAY MCLEAN: AUSTRALIAN JACK-OF-ALL-TRADES, FORMER engineer and proofreader for a women's magazine, can fix anything.

LATICIA WOLFE, A.K.A. "THE WIDOW": EMACIATED BUT HARD A tempered steel, only hope is that her son will grow up to be a strong, capable man.

PAUL WOLFE, 11, A YOUNG MAN GROWING STRONGER THANKS TO the rigors of frontier life and help from Heck and Seeker.

BURT BICKLE: FREIGHTER, HARD WORKER, AMBITIOUS.

ABE ZALE: YOUNG WOODCUTTER WITH A CAN-DO ATTITUDE.

A.J. PLUM: TALENTED BLACKSMITH, STUBBORN, GETS AN IDEA AND sticks to it. With him are his wife and three children, the oldest of which is nine-year-old Martin, a good little carpenter.

. . .

GABLE PILLSBURY: FARMER.

VERONICA PILLSBURY: EXPERIENCED MIDWIFE, GABLE'S WIFE, mother of two children.

FRANK PILLSBURY: FARMER, GABLE'S BROTHER, HUSBAND OF DOT, father of four children including thirteen-year-old Franky and eleven-year-old Mary.

WILL AYERS: CARPENTER.

CHAPTER 1

D.J. Weller chuckled as he uprooted the sign and tossed it to the ground.

Heck's Valley, the sign read. *Private property. 24 square miles. Visitors are welcome. Trespassers are not. No prospecting, no panning. Owners: Seeker Yates, Hope Martin, Heck Martin.*

"Well, that was easy enough," D.J.'s brother, Lyle, said. "Best get rid of that sign altogether."

"Later. Let's stake our claim first."

D.J. held their sign, and Lyle went to work with the hammer, pounding away with little effect. For as easy as it was to uproot the original, they had an awful hard time trying to stake their own claim.

"Get her in there, Lyle," D.J. said.

"Cain't," Lyle grunted. "They's a rock."

"Maybe it's a hundred-pound nugget of gold," D.J. joked.

The men's laughter broke off when a voice spoke behind them.

"You boys stop what you're doing and don't do anything stupid. I don't want to shoot you."

D.J. whirled around and felt a stab of fear.

Before them stood a gigantic man. He looked about seven feet tall to D.J. His hair was as black as midnight, and his eyes blazed like blue fire.

"It's him," Lyle said, "the one Boon talked about."

No stranger to trouble, the brothers spread out.

D.J. had figured it would come to this but hadn't counted on Martin finding them so quickly.

He sure was big. Oh well, they weren't looking to wrestle the man. A .36 caliber slug went through meat like it was grits.

"Boon?" Martin said, sounding irritated. "Trace Boon?"

"That's right, Mister," D.J. said, letting his hand settle on the butt of his pistol. "He told us all about the big nugget."

"Yeah," Lyle said. "Where you got the rest of your gold?"

"Get your hands off your guns," Martin said. If he was scared, he sure did hide it well. "I don't want to kill you."

"Who said anything about killing?" D.J. said, and licked his lips, which were suddenly dry as dust.

"Go!" Lyle shouted.

In a panic, D.J. realized his brother was drawing—

But that realization shattered beneath the impossibly loud explosion not of Lyle's pistol but Martin's.

Some part of D.J.'s mind understood his brother was down, hit hard, maybe even dead—a shocking notion that filled D.J. with terror... as did the realization of just how quickly Martin had gotten his gun into action.

D.J. tugged at his own weapon, but the world around him seemed to have sped up. His movements felt slow, like something out of a nightmare, and he was still shucking his Navy Colt when Heck Martin turned the smoking barrel in D.J.'s direction and walked forward, shaking his head with something like disgust.

The boom of Martin's pistol chased its bright flash. D.J.'s chest exploded with pain, and he collapsed into the arms of death.

CHAPTER 2

"Warned you," Heck told the dead men. "I didn't want to kill you."

He shook his head and looked at their broken bodies. Their empty eyes stared up at the clouds.

Heck spat on the ground.

He was tired of digging graves for these trespassers. Seemed like Jem and Trace had traveled half the West, telling everyone they met about Heck's gold.

Someday, he knew, a bigger crew would come along. And then what?

Well, he'd deal with them, too.

But he sure did look forward to the day they stopped coming. At some point, wouldn't they wise up?

Old timber towered on all sides. This time of year, the big trees cast cool shade. Because the trees were spread apart, however, shafts of bright summer sunlight fell between the pools of shadow, sparkling with motes of dust and pollen.

Standing within one of those sparkling shafts, Heck turned, studying the land below this ridge.

To the north, he saw the Oregon Trail running east toward Fort Laramie and west toward the mountains where Seeker's uncle, Black Cloud, and his Shoshone tribe lived. Further west, about a hundred miles from Heck, was Fort Bridger, where Heck's friends, Jim Bridger and Two Bits, ran the next trading post on the long trip to the West Coast.

Turning to the east, he could see his home, Heck's Valley, where he lived with his wife, Hope; their son, Tor; his adopted brother, Seeker; and Hope's family—Mr. and Mrs. Mullen; their son, Tom; and his new wife, Amelia—along with the ever-growing population of Hope City, which had developed significantly over the year since Heck had returned from San Francisco, where he had sold the massive nugget and recaptured the title of heavyweight boxing champion of the West while narrowly escaping some very bad men.

Don Vasquez's payment for the nugget had come in the form of twelve hundred longhorns, a dozen top-notch cattle horses, and six months of service from Vasquez's experienced vaqueros, who had driven the cattle up from Mexico, gotten them settled, then taught Heck and his friends the ins and outs of tending the herd, keeping it healthy, and helping it to grow.

Farther to the south, he could see longhorns grazing in the first of the grassy valleys, their colorful hides bright in the sunlight. It was almost time to move them south again to the open range.

Among the cattle, men moved on horseback. Heck and his friends had learned a lot from the vaqueros and had learned even more dealing with the realities of running so many cattle in this bountiful land.

It was hard work, but Heck loved it. They had kept the long-horns alive through all sorts of weather, birthed calves, cut steers, and even shipped a hundred head two hundred miles to Fort Laramie, where Heck's old friend and the fort's top supply officer, Major Avery Scottsdale, purchased the steers for a good price.

But the herd was mostly young stuff, so Heck would wait for next spring before doing a big push to Fort Laramie, knowing four and five-year-old steers would bring a better price.

And if he wanted to make his investment pay, he needed to earn top dollar.

Which, truth be told, he no longer needed, but he would not allow God's bounty to make him slothful.

Besides, out here in the wilderness, money wasn't quite so real as it was back in civilization.

Cows were real. Land was real. People were real. But most of the time, money was merely an idea.

He would continue to live as he always had—nose to ground, working hard—watch his pennies, and try to pass on that work ethic and mindset to his son, Tor, and the baby Hope now carried in her womb.

They were so blessed.

Glancing back at the dead men lying twisted on the ridge, he shook his head again.

Shame that blessings so frequently invited curses.

CHAPTER 3

"D addy!" Tor hollered and came pounding across the cabin floor.

Tor was tall for fifteen months and healthy with Heck's black hair and his mother's bright green eyes. The boy had walked at nine months. Now, he ran everywhere he went, pounding the world beneath his feet with choppy steps.

Like his father, Tor woke quickly and charged into the day. Then, when it was time to sleep, he crashed so hard that Heck reckoned he could sleep through a gun battle.

Heck swept Tor into his arms.

The boy's laughter broke Heck's heart with love.

"Daddy home!"

Heck gave him a bounce then set him back down. "That's right, little man. I'm home for a bit."

"Yay!" Tor shouted and sped across the cabin. Coming back at full speed, he fell pretty hard. Sitting up, Tor rubbed his head and looked to his mother.

"You're all right, Tor," Hope said with a smile. She was a loving mother but never coddled. "Get up."

Tor grinned, got to his feet, and zipped away again.

"See anything up on the ridge?" Hope asked.

Heck went to the coffee pot and poured a mug and took a sip. It was still hot. "Yes, ma'am, I sure did."

She knew him well. "Oh no, again?"

He nodded.

She shook her head. "Long way to come just to get killed."

"Yeah, well, it seems to be a popular notion."

"How many does that make?"

"Eleven. Every last one of them tipped off by Jem Pulcher and Trace Boon."

Hope's brow wrinkled with anger. "Lot of blood on their hands."

He nodded. "Lot of blood. Makes a man question his notions of mercy."

"What do you mean?"

"Remember when they broke into our cabin, and we let them go?"

"I do."

"I keep thinking if I'd shot them instead, it would've saved eleven lives."

"Well, don't think about it too much, Heck. You did the right thing, showing mercy. Some folks are just bad all the way through."

"It's true. But I wish Trace and Jem would quit sending people here."

Hope nodded. "I'm just glad these prospectors are only

showing up in twos and threes. I hate to think of you facing eleven at once."

"That might be a problem. Honestly, I'm surprised it hasn't happened already."

"Do you think it will?"

Standing in the open door of the cabin, he sipped the coffee, looking out at the opposite slope of the valley beyond the walls of Fort Seeker. "Yeah, I guess maybe I reckon it will."

Hope shifted in her seat, frowning. "I hope you're wrong about that, Heck."

"I hope I am, too. But I doubt it."

"What'll we do if they do come? In a big group, I mean."

"They come, they'll wish they hadn't. We risked everything to buy this valley, build the town, and bring in the longhorns. I'm gonna do whatever it takes to make that gamble pay off."

"And I'll be right at your side," Hope said.

"I know you will," Heck said. "And with you at my side, I'll face anything."

Of course, neither of them knew then what was riding their way at that moment, drawing closer every day...

CHAPTER 4

A week later, the real trouble started.

Heck had just finished talking with his friend, Doctor Michael Skiff, and Doc's fiancé, Miss Aya Sion, an attractive blond-haired woman with a great sense of humor and a fearsome temper. Heck was looking up the road, impressed as always by how much Hope City had grown over the last year, when a wagonload of rough-looking men came rolling into view.

They stopped and hollered a question about the trading post, and someone pointed past Heck toward the picketed walls of Fort Seeker.

The men looked like prospectors to Heck. And lo and behold, as they creaked past, the newcomers studied everything with glittering eyes, not just the people and businesses but also the cliffs and river and surrounding country.

The gates of Fort Seeker stood open.

The wagon rolled through them.

"Them boys look like trouble," Dusty Maguire said. Maguire, an experienced cowboy and all-around good man, had ridden in with the vaqueros, fallen in love with the valley, and opted to stay.

"I was thinking the same thing," Heck said. "Let's mosey on over in case they stir up something."

They didn't have to wait long.

In fact, by the time they ambled through the gate, they already heard rough laughter and a deep voice bellowing, "How about I put my fist through your face?"

Veronica Pillsbury, the midwife who'd delivered Heck's son, came running over with a panicked expression. "Come quick, Heck. There are some men who are being awfully rude. They're giving Wyatt Henley a terrible time."

Wyatt Henley was another newcomer. He'd arrived a couple of months earlier. A talkative, inquisitive man, he seemed to be interested in everything and lent a hand wherever one was needed: hunting, gathering firewood, watching cattle, or pitching in with whatever building folks were putting up.

Now, he was the one who needed help.

"I don't want trouble, sir," Wyatt told a hulking man in a faded red shirt. "I already apologized—even though I never did anything in the first place."

"You calling me a liar?" the big man shouted, and shoved Wyatt to the ground.

A circle of onlookers, mostly women and children, gasped at the sudden violence.

"Get up and let me knock you down good and proper," the big man sneered.

His friends—Heck saw four men in total, but there could be

more in the wagon—laughed like they'd never heard anything so funny.

"Leave him alone," Heck warned.

The men turned toward Heck. Their expressions surprised him. They not only looked like they recognized him but like they had been expecting him.

"You gonna make me?" the big one said. Reaching under the buckboard, he brought out a short cudgel of dark wood. "I'll knock your brains out, buddy."

Ten paces away, Heck slid the Colt from his belt. "Go ahead and try."

Beside him, Maguire filled his hand with iron, too.

And not just Maguire. All around the courtyard, barrels rose. Even Veronica Pillsbury pointed a tiny derringer at the man with the club.

Hope City had its ways. And its citizens would stand together.

Wyatt climbed to his feet and stepped back, dusting himself off and watching the big man nervously.

The big man laughed, ignoring everyone but Heck. "You're lucky you got that gun."

"Is that right?" Heck said. "Throw down your club, and we'll put our guns away."

The other men grinned at the big guy, and Heck was struck by the feeling—almost a certainty—that none of this was by chance. These men had been waiting for this moment, hoping for it.

Something was going on here, something calculated.

Who were these men? Why did the burly, gap-toothed man tossing away his cudgel and rolling up his sleeves look so pleased?

"There," the man said. "No club. Now, are you a man of your word or a coward?"

"You've come to the wrong place, bearing talk like that," Heck said, handing his pistol to Maguire and walking forward. "Out here, folks hold you accountable for your words."

The man in the red shirt came forward, too, tightening his big hands into fists. "Where I come from, we let our fists do the talking."

"Get him, Denny!" the other men shouted.

"Keep an eye on the others," Heck whispered to Maguire. "I don't trust them."

Maguire nodded.

Denny launched a sloppy but powerful haymaker. There was no subtlety in it, no feint or clever footwork. He just surged ahead, grunting as he hurled his massive fist at Heck's head.

Heck slipped the punch easily and buried an uppercut in Denny's hard stomach, which gave beneath Heck's knuckles, forcing another grunt from the burly man.

Heck took a few steps to one side and waited for the charge.

With a cry of rage, Denny rushed forward, throwing desperate hooks.

Heck punched straight between the hooks, stepping back as he pumped his left jab two, three, four times, pulping Denny's nose, splitting his lip, and cracking open one eyebrow.

The big man paused for a second, clearly shocked by the last few seconds.

"Had enough?" Heck asked.

With another bellow, Denny rushed forward.

Heck stepped to one side, held out a boot, and tripped him.

Denny crashed into the dust, already huffing and puffing, darkening the dust with drops of blood. Frustrated, he slammed a palm into the ground and got to his feet again.

"Smash him, Denny!" the other men shouted. "Knock his teeth out!"

Heck's mind whirred along, analyzing everything the way it did whenever trouble was at hand.

Who were these men? What did they want? Clearly, they wanted to find and hurt Heck.

But why?

Did he know them?

He didn't think so, and he had a good memory for faces.

Denny came at him again, bent low, arms out, going for a tackle.

Heck knew better than to wrestle with this bull-necked opponent. That would play to Denny's strengths and allow him to get close, where he might gouge Heck's eye or bite off Heck's finger or ear or nose.

So Heck sidestepped the attack.

Denny came back at him, still bent low, arms outstretched. His face was wide open.

Unwilling to bust his knuckles, Heck lashed out with a stomping kick. His bootheel slammed into Denny's forehead, stopped him dead in his tracks, and dropped him to the ground like a poleaxed calf.

Denny twitched a little, but it was just his nerves. The big man was out cold and would have a wall banger of a headache whenever he finally woke up.

The other men stared in shocked silence.

"Pick him up and get out of here," Heck told them. "You're not welcome in this valley."

"Not so," a familiar voice said from behind Heck. "These men are with me."

Heck turned, saw who was coming, and could not believe his eyes.

CHAPTER 5

It was Percival Dumay, the richest man in California.

Heck hadn't seen him since that day in the graveyard, when Dumay had outbid Vasquez, but Heck had sold the nugget to the cattleman anyway.

Dumay vowed to get even with Heck.

Now he was here with these troublemakers and a dozen other hard-looking men. Most of them were young and muscular and putting too much into their sneering expressions.

One, however, stood out. A lean, thirtyish man in a black suit and a flat-crowned, black hat eyed Heck intently but without malice, his pale blue eyes sparkling with keen interest. Radiating calm confidence, he wore a pistol on both hips—not shoved into the belt, like most folks—but within leather holsters, the bottoms of which were tied down to his thighs with leather strings.

Dumay lifted his chin a little, showing Heck a superior

smile. "What's the matter, Mr. Martin? Don't you remember me?"

"I remember you, Mr. Dumay," Heck said. "I'm just trying to figure out what you're doing here, so far from home."

"When you cheated me out of the golden nugget," Dumay said, his smile faltering slightly, "I told you that you hadn't heard the last of me."

Heck nodded. "I remember. You were quite upset."

Dumay spread his hands. "It was a disappointment. But I don't get angry, Mr. Martin. I get even."

"Long way to come just to settle a score," Heck said, trying to read the situation. Whatever these men were fixing to do, they had to notice all the guns surrounding them. "What do you have in mind?"

"I'm going to mine this valley, of course."

Heck raised one brow. "Too late. I own this ground."

"Correction, Mr. Martin," Dumay said. "You own the surface, but I own everything beneath our feet, not to mention a good deal of the surrounding country."

"What are you talking about?"

"Your lawyer—Dean, was it?—wasn't nearly so good as you thought he was. He secured this godforsaken acreage for you, but he paid no attention to the accompanying mineral rights— which I now own."

"I don't believe it."

"No? Read this, then," Dumay said, and handed Heck an envelope. "You'll see that I own everything beneath the surface of your valley, including any gold or silver you might have discovered in recent months."

Heck stuffed the envelope into his pocket. "How did you even find me?"

"I had the counsel of mutual acquaintances," Dumay said. "Men, come forward and say hello to your old friend, Mr. Martin."

Heck's hackles rose as two men who had been very much on his mind of late stepped from behind the others.

Trace Boon looked embarrassed and frightened.

His cousin, Jem Pulcher, grinned like a rat in a cheese cellar.

"You dirty snakes," Heck said. "After all I did for you, saving you from death and showing you mercy when you broke into my cabin, this is the thanks I get?"

"Don't be sore, Heck," Jem said, still grinning nastily. "Mr. Dumay's been real nice to us. Helping him was the least we could do."

"What about all the others you helped? A bunch of them have shown up here, hunting gold, throwing your names around."

Trace Boon's eyes swelled at that.

Jem just laughed. "Small timers. If they're hanging around, tell 'em they'd best clear out. The real operation is here now."

"They're not going anywhere," Heck said.

"Oh yes, they are," Dumay said. "The mining rights I hold are exclusive. Everything beneath the surface is mine and mine alone."

"Well, if that's true, you own these other gold hunters, too. They're buried upon the ridge. Unless the wolves dug them up."

This knocked the smile off Jem's face.

"Whatever the case, you have been served notice of my ownership and intentions," Dumay said. "Within a week's time, my men will require the use of this road. We have a significant amount of mining equipment, as you might guess."

"You're talking a lot of nonsense, Dumay. Get off our land and don't come back. I'll tell you what I told your thugs. You're not welcome here."

"Now," Dumay said, ignoring Heck and pointing across the courtyard toward the Mullens' home, which was built into the cliffside, "it's my understanding that one accesses the caves through that... whatever it is."

"I told you to get out," Heck said, and took a step forward.

Startled, Dumay stepped backward. His thugs bristled.

Not the man in black, though. He just continued to study Heck with cool confidence.

"Read the affidavit," Dumay said. "You'll see that everything is in order. And frankly, Mr. Martin, even if it weren't in order, there would be little you could do to stop us. How many people live in this ridiculous little village? A hundred? Fewer, I'd guess. And of those, how many able-bodied men? Thirty-five? Forty?"

Heck just stared at him.

"I'm bringing in one hundred and twenty-seven strong men. I'm going to exercise my mineral rights and extract every last ounce of gold, even if I have to turn this whole valley into a massive crater. We will return by way of this convenient road and begin a large-scale mining operation. You can step aside or get plowed like a turnip field, your choice."

Heck gave him a hard look. "You try to plow over us, Dumay, you're gonna find we're a rocky field."

CHAPTER 6

As Dumay and his men departed, Heck's neighbors stepped aside, letting them pass, their expressions showing anger, confusion, and fear.

Heck wondered what was going on here. Could Dumay really have purchased the mineral rights underneath him? And if so, what did that mean, exactly? In all his reading, he had never come across anything about that.

Dumay sure had seemed confident. Victorious, even.

Dusty Maguire stepped up to Heck. The tough cowboy looked concerned. "You see that fella in black?"

Heck nodded. "Seemed like a pretty cool character."

"That's one way to put it. You don't know him?"

"Nope."

"That was Frank Wedge."

"Never heard of him."

Maguire looked at him curiously. "He's famous."

"For what?"

"Killing folks."

"Hmm. That explains the guns."

"That's all you got to say? The way you and that Dumay was talking, I thought maybe the lead would start flying."

"It didn't."

"Lucky for you. Wedge is known all over the West. He's deadlier than cholera. Last I heard, he'd killed thirty-some men."

"That's a lot of people."

Maguire squinted at him. "You're kind of peculiar sometimes, my friend."

"You're not the first person to say something along those lines."

People flooded into the courtyard, everyone talking at once, wanting to know what happened.

Among them was Hope. She had been visiting with Amelia, who now had a cabin with Hope's brother, Tom, in town. Hope came briskly forward, approaching Heck with Tor in her arms and a grave expression on her pretty face. She looked neither worried nor fearful—Hope had total faith in her husband—but clearly understood something serious had transpired.

"What happened?" she asked, reaching him.

"Daddy!" Tor shouted.

Taking his son into his arms, Heck told Hope what had happened.

"Is that possible?" Hope asked. "What he said, about the mineral rights?"

"I don't even know. He handed me an envelope. Said there's an affidavit inside. Let's go inside and give it a read."

But the citizens of Hope City were too riled up for Heck and his little family to retreat just yet.

People passed the name Frank Wedge back and forth, sounding scared.

Dumay's claim of one hundred and twenty-seven men coming into the valley was also repeated on all sides.

"I've heard of this man Dumay," Titus Haines, the schoolmaster, said. "He's quite wealthy."

"Richest man West of the Mississippi," someone said.

"Question is, what does he want with us?" Doc said. "Gold?"

Heck nodded. "That's part of it. But I reckon there's more to it than that."

Everyone was silent now, waiting for him to speak.

Looking out at their faces, he realized that many of these people, perhaps even most, had arrived since his return from San Francisco, so he briefly explained the nugget and some of what had happened there, wrapping up with the auction. "I knew he was angry when I sold the nugget to Vasquez. In fact, Dumay told me I hadn't heard the last of him. I just never dreamed he'd come all this way to get even."

"It does seem like a lot of trouble, especially for a man of his wealth and station. Why bother?"

"Must've been even madder than you thought," Maguire volunteered.

"Do you really think he'll do it?" the still dusty Wyatt Henley asked. "Bring all those men in here, plow us like a turnip field?"

"I reckon he'll try," Heck said.

A ripple of fear burbled through the crowd.

"They can try," said A.J. Plum, who looked formidable, standing there, clutching his blacksmith's hammer, his face fierce with anger, his sweat-soaked clothes clinging to his muscular frame.

"That's right, A.J.," Heck said. "And if they try, they're gonna be in for quite a surprise. We can't afford an all-out war with that many men, but if they try to push into our valley, we have to be ready to hit them hard and drive them off."

"Are you sure that's wise, Heck?" Veronica Pillsbury said. "They look like awfully hard men."

Wyatt Henley and several others nodded.

"What are you proposing?" Burt Bickle, the town's biggest employer asked. "You think we should just step aside and let them have the valley?"

"Couldn't we parlay?" Veronica asked. Several frightened-looking people nodded, clearly agreeing with her. "Talk things over, come to an agreement?"

Burt shook his head. "I worked too hard building Bickle Freighting to hand it over to a bunch of thugs."

"Same here," A.J. Plum said, hefting his big hammer. "I will stand and fight."

"Against one hundred and twenty-seven men?" Wyatt said. "Like Veronica said, they're very rough. How would we even resist them?" He turned to Heck. "What would your defensive plan be against so many?"

"I'll talk to a few people and figure that out," Heck said. "First, we need to do some scouting. I want to know where these people are and what they're up to. But as to these men being tough, there are a lot of different types of tough. Some men are tigers with their hands but lambs as soon as a gun goes off. Other men are the toughest, meanest people you've ever seen—until they get punched in the nose. These men strike me as being cut of that cloth. If they come in here, trying to intimidate us, we'll haul off and slug them in the nose and see how tough they really are."

"Big risk," someone said.

"I suppose," Heck said, and swept his gaze over the crowd, making eye contact with several men he knew well, "but I know we're tough. We drove off the Sioux raiders. And if these men want to fight, we'll drive them off, too."

The men he'd made eye contact with nodded in agreement. Several others did, too.

"We're not just defending our land and property," Heck said, and gave Tor a bounce. "We're defending our way of life, our freedom, and our families. And those are things I'd rather die for than surrender."

CHAPTER 7

Dumay sat on the buckboard with Frank Wedge, sipping coffee and waiting for the men to set up his tent, which he would use until they finished building him a proper cabin.

This would be the first of many buildings in Dumay's southernmost valley, which was about three miles from Heck Martin's property line.

Dumay sipped his coffee and scanned the huge valley, its waving stand of green grass, and the high, jagged peaks that rose on both sides.

From the reports he'd received, if he followed wagon ruts just a bit north of this point, he could drive a wagon up the series of linked valleys with no trouble at all, connect to Heck Martin's road, and be in Hope City in under an hour.

But it had taken them a good portion of the morning and the whole afternoon to travel from Hope City back up to the Oregon Trail, backtrack around the mountains, and head south to this point over rough ground.

The ride had been slow and bumpy and infuriating. Dumay had started out in a state of near elation, slid in and out of anger, and now sat in sullen exhaustion.

"What does anyone see in country like this?" he demanded.

Frank Wedge spread his capable hands. "Some folks like it. I can recognize a certain stark beauty, but me, I've always been more of a town man."

"Well, after we drive these sodbusters out of here, you can have any house you like in Hope City."

Wedge shook his head. "Once my work's done, I'm heading east."

"You'll have enough to retire."

"I already had enough to retire."

"If you don't need the money, Mr. Wedge, why are you here?"

"It's what I do."

"Yes, for money. But if you already have all the money you need—"

"Like I said, it's what I do. You might even say it's who I am."

"A killer."

Wedge turned his pale blue eyes on Dumay and blinked slowly. "I solve problems other men can't. And from what I understand, this Heck Martin is a sizeable problem. I have to say, he does strike me as a fighter."

"A boxer. But that's not what we're doing here. There is no ring, no referee, no rules."

"Well, there are some rules."

Dumay made a face. "Rules? What rules?"

Wedge raised a hand. "They don't concern you. It's just that these sorts of conflicts should be carried out in an orderly fashion. I prefer a duel over cold-blooded murder."

"Well, I don't think it will come to either. For as much as I'm determined to drive off these fools, I'd rather not kill them. Unless something changes, you are my personal bodyguard, nothing more."

"Something will change, though."

"Why do you say that?"

"Heck Martin."

"What about him?"

"He's a fighter. He won't just pull up his tent pegs and vanish. He'll take some pushing."

"Well, if that yokel thinks he can keep me out of his valley, he's in for a big surprise."

Wedge said nothing, just staring at Dumay with those unnerving eyes.

"The rest of the men and the mining equipment should be here within a week," Dumay said. "We'll let them rest a little, feed them some beef, then march down that road in full force."

"This should be interesting. The men have been talking tough nonstop since California. Now, we'll see how tough they really are."

"Oh, they're plenty tough, Mr. Wedge. I assure you. My agents gathered only the toughest."

"We'll see."

"You don't sound very confident in your colleagues."

"They're not my colleagues."

"You both work for me."

"They are not my colleagues. They are loudmouthed bruisers."

"Exactly. Perfect for busting up a town and scaring off its citizenry."

"Perhaps. But some citizenry doesn't scare so easily. Want me to call out Heck Martin first?" Wedge asked as naturally as he might offer to hold a door for someone carrying a stack of firewood.

Dumay looked at him strangely, surprised again by this oddly composed man, for whom killing seemed no more unsettling than combing his hair or perhaps brushing a speck of mud from his shoes.

"No, I do not want you to call out Heck Martin. As I've told you, it won't come to that. I've gone to great lengths and great expense to avoid barbarism."

"The affidavit."

"That's part of it."

"Is it real?"

"Real enough to get the job done. In business, my dear Mr. Wedge, timing is everything."

"The same could be said about my business."

"Then you will understand. If I waited around any longer, Heck Martin might have sold his claim to another company and ruined everything. My lawyers are hard at work, trying to solidify my claim. The affidavit will work for now, and now is what we're concerned with. By the time anyone back in civilization questions anything with real scrutiny, we already will have ruined Martin, driven him off, and taken possession of his valley, his town, and his gold."

"Just like that, huh?"

"Yes, just like that. And trust me, everything is in order. If things go less smoothly than expected, we will move to the next stage of the plan."

Feeling triumphant, he patted the breast pocket where he kept the all-important envelope. But that, he would not share with Wedge or anyone else—not until he delivered it to the very important person to whom it was addressed.

If it came to that...

Dumay grinned.

If it came to that, Martin wouldn't stand a chance.

CHAPTER 8

"I should've bought this ground when I had the chance," Heck muttered a week later, lying on his belly atop the ridge, staring down at Dumay's field through spyglasses. Bright green grass swayed in the breeze.

"Well," Dusty Maguire said, "trouble is that your back trail ain't your back trail till it is. I reckon what you did seemed like a good idea at the time."

"It did," Heck said.

"We ought to unload on 'em," Seeker said.

"No, we oughtn't, little brother. We are not starting a shooting war with these people."

"I don't mean kill 'em, Heck. I could just put one through the bottom of that fella's pan down there, give him a little scare."

Far below, the valley thrummed with action. More wagons were arriving along with more men like those who'd accompanied Dumay the day he'd visited the valley to bluster and threaten.

40

Most of these men were hard at work building log cabins and barns and corrals. A dozen, however—including the man to whom Seeker referred—crouched alongside the river, panning for gold.

So far, none of them seemed to have found even a spot of color.

Whatever else they were doing, they were causing Heck trouble.

For all Dumay's tough talk, neither he nor his men had stepped foot in Hope City since that first day. But their mere presence here was a powerful disruption.

Right now, Heck was more concerned about grass than gold.

Then Seeker, whose thoughts so frequently paralleled his own, said, "That's our grass down there."

"Is it, though? Dumay said he bought the surrounding country. What if that's his grass now?"

In country such as this, with good, rich forage, you needed around four acres of grass per longhorn. With 1200 head to fatten up, Heck needed the ground south of his property, including this valley.

Otherwise, even if he fenced off pasture sections and ran the cattle on a rotational grazing schedule, he'd overgraze his own land. If that happened, the grass would suffer.

The cows' hooves would tear things up, then rain and flooding would erode the damaged ground, and he'd lose topsoil. Meaning next spring, he'd be running a skinny herd, and skinny steers sold for far less than fat ones.

There was more grass in the upper meadows and higher up among the old timber, but would it be enough?

For now, perhaps. But not next spring, when the herd grew, especially if the valley grass suffered.

And that could add up to Heck losing his big gamble.

For now, while the grass closer to home replenished itself, Heck's herd was grazing in the big valley between his valley and this one.

So far, Dumay was only running a small herd down there, twenty-five head by Heck's count, and keeping them close to his camp.

"When you reckon he's gonna make a move?" Maguire asked.

"I have no idea," Heck said.

"I don't believe anything he says," Seeker declared. "He's a liar. Said he was bringing in a hundred and twenty-seven men to knock heads. Shoot. There ain't but fifty-some down there."

"Fifty-seven by count," Heck said. "Though there could be a few inside that we can't see."

"Call it sixty, then," Seeker said. "Sixty ain't a hundred and twenty-seven."

"No, it's not," Heck said. "But don't forget the men up by the trail."

A few days earlier, after hearing rumors from passing emigrants stopping by the post, they had scouted to the north and discovered a second encampment of Dumay's men camping alongside the Oregon Trail, in a meadow beside the river a quarter mile west of where the road to Heck's intersected the trail. There weren't many of them, but there were nearly a dozen wagons mostly loaded, Heck guessed, with mining equipment.

"What are there, ten of them? Sixty plus ten ain't a hundred and twenty-seven, Heck."

"No, but I got a hunch Dumay has something up his sleeve. Let's go on up there and see what those other men are up to."

They crawled back from the edge and got their horses and mounted up and rode north through the widespread trees and meadows topping the ridge until they came to its northernmost limits, where, peering down, they beheld a shocking sight.

"Look at 'em all," Seeker said, sounding disgusted.

"Thick as flies on a turd, ain't they?" Maguire said.

Heck nodded, counting the men and wagons who had only recently joined Dumay's northern camp a quarter mile west of the road to Heck's Valley.

"Well, there's the rest of Dumay's men he promised. There's seventy of them down there, maybe more."

It was hard to say just how many men there were because they never quit moving.

He lifted his spyglasses and watched them for a while.

These men were miners, too. Most were short and rugged with drooping mustaches, red shirts, and small, dark caps atop their heads. Many carried rifles or had a pistol shoved into their pants.

They were very rough and rowdy and made so much noise, he could hear their shouting and laughter and an occasional gunshot from all the way up here.

"Looks like maybe Dumay wasn't lying after all," Seeker conceded.

"Yeah," Heck said. "His army's here. And my guess is we're gonna get a close look at them real soon."

"Wouldn't otherwise be much sense in bringing so many

men over such a long distance, would there?" Maguire said from atop his horse. The wiry cowboy leaned and spat on the ground. "Question is, what are we gonna do about it?"

"We can't afford a full-out war with these people," Heck said again. He found himself saying that all the time, both to others and himself. This was a new situation for him. "There are too many of them, and we're too vulnerable."

"You got that right," Maguire agreed. "Them boys down there don't look like polished soldiers. They look more like the type to get drunk and bust up a saloon. They start pitching lead, it'll go all over the place. And bullets don't care who they kill—man, woman, or child."

CHAPTER 9

Dumay paced back and forth, loving the feel of the floorboards beneath his clean shoes.

His consultants had questioned the idea of dedicating an entire wagon to planking, but Dumay had explained in no uncertain terms that, while he was prepared to do without certain creature comforts, he would not wallow in the mud like a pig.

After ten days in this godforsaken valley, he believed that bringing planking along had been one of his greatest ideas ever, right up there with running McCardle out of the Tuppence Mine or investing the fortune he'd made there on Nob Hill real estate and the various San Francisco businesses through which he had multiplied his enormous fortune many times over by selling overpriced miners with a surplus of gold dust and a dearth of everything else, including brains.

A fool and his money are soon parted, they said, and Dumay

had made a towering fortune off that truism. Now, the biggest fool of them all, Heck Martin, was about to add to that fortune.

Frank Wedge leaned against the wall, near the door, his pale blue eyes shifting from Dumay to the three men seated at the table.

Jem Pulcher rocked back on the legs of the chair in which he was sitting and passed the whiskey flask to his cousin, Trace Boon.

Dumay neither liked nor trusted the pair, but he wanted them present while planning the next move. They had, after all, lived with the citizens of Hope City for many months.

So far, however, the other person at the table had been doing all the talking, which made Dumay happy he'd hired the man to come out months earlier and live and work alongside Heck Martin and the others.

"They're scared," Wyatt Henley said. "Not Heck, of course, but most of them are downright terrified. They've been scared since you showed up, but now, after hearing about the rest of your men showing up? They're petrified." He shook his head, laughing. "You should hear them whine."

"That would be funny," Jem said, and took another slug of whiskey. "Is Plum scared? I sure hope so. I hate him."

"Plum?" Wyatt said. "Not a chance. I don't think it's possible to scare that man."

"What defenses do they have planned?" Wedge asked from his position beside the door.

Wyatt shrugged. "I asked Heck a couple of times, but he didn't say much. Just that they would keep an eye, and if anyone sees us coming, the women and children are supposed to get inside the fort."

"We oughta bring most of the men down the trail, let them brace up, then sneak into the fort and take the women and children hostage," Jem said. "See how tough Heck is when I got a knife to his boy's throat."

Wedge came off the wall. "Get out."

Jem set all four chair legs on the ground and half turned, eyes bulging. "Me?"

"Yes, you," Wedge said. "Out. Now."

"Why?"

"Because I'm not going to stand here and listen to any more of your barbaric ideas."

Jem made a face but stood to leave. He cast one last look at Dumay, probably hoping for a reprieve, but Dumay did not intervene.

Wedge was right. Jem Pulcher was a coarse man, and his presence grated like an iron file.

"I'm not telling you again," Wedge said. He put a hand on one of his pistols, and his pale eyes darkened.

Jem held up his hands. "All right, all right. I'm going." Halfway out the door, he rolled his eyes and took his parting shot at Wedge. "Barbaric ideas? I thought you was supposed to be some big killer."

"You want to try me?" Wedge asked.

Jem shook his head and called to his cousin.

Trace Boon hurried after him, offering a ridiculous little bow on the way out.

Wedge closed the door behind them and spoke to Wyatt Henley. "Are you telling us that's it? The men have no specific defense planned?"

"No, that's not it," Wyatt said. "They just didn't tell me was all. Heck talked it over with his closest friends, the ones he's fought with before, you understand, and didn't say word one to the rest of us."

"He must suspect something," Wedge said.

"Hmm. Could be," Dumay said. "Do you think he suspects you?"

"Me?" Wyatt said. "No. Not at all. Why would he? I've done nothing but help the whole time I was there. Then your idea about having Creighton smack me around... well, it hurt, and I wouldn't want to have to go through it again, but it was smart, that's for sure."

"Whom does he trust?" Wedge asked. "Tell me about them."

"There's a bunch of them. Mostly, he leans on his family, especially his wife, Hope, and his little brother, Seeker. Don't let that kid fool you. He might only be thirteen, but he's as deadly as you. Well, maybe not, but you get my point. The boy is a killer."

Wedge nodded, taking it all in.

"He's close with Doc—Doc Skiff, that is; he's the local sawbones. Also, the Australian guy who fixes everything, Ray McLean, and the woodcutter, Abe Zale. He can shoot. And one of Vasquez's vaqueros who stayed on, Dusty Maguire. He's so skinny he barely throws a shadow on a bright day, but don't underestimate him, either. He's been around, and he's good with firearms. Rifles and pistols both."

Wedge nodded. "Who else?"

"Well, those are Heck's main confidantes, along with Hope's family, like I said. Her dad, her brother. Then, there's a bunch of others Heck trusts. Guys he's known for a while, guys he's fought alongside. Like the blacksmith and that kid, Paul Wolfe."

"Tell me about all of them," Wedge said.

"All right, I will," Wyatt said, "but I think you're worrying too much about all this. I'm telling you, these people are scared. Now is the time to push."

"He might be right," Dumay said. "Besides, the men are growing restless. Men like these, you can't let them sit too long or they start fighting among themselves."

"They've already started," Wedge said.

"It's bad for morale," Dumay said. "I think we should gather everyone together and go pay Mr. Martin a visit."

Wyatt grinned at that. "They'll get right out of your way, and the road will be yours. First the road, then the gold."

"Just like that, huh?" Wedge said.

"Yeah," Wyatt said, "just like that. Look, I've been living with these people for months. I know them. And they are ready to buckle."

"All of them?"

"Enough. Folks start running, that'll break the ones who might otherwise stand."

Dumay nods. "That's true. It's human nature."

Wedge chuckled. "Neither of you see what I see."

Dumay felt a twinge of irritation at Wedge's smugness. "And what, precisely, do you see?"

"I see at least a handful of men down there with no quit in them. No quit whatsoever. And topping that list is Heck Martin."

Wyatt nodded. "Truth be told, he does have guts. But how can one man make a difference against so many?"

"You wait and see," Wedge said. "It will all come down to Heck Martin—and the difference he makes."

"You are oversimplifying the situation, Mr. Wedge," Dumay said. "Trust me. I arranged everything in my favor. I didn't bring all these men to wage a war. I brought them to make a statement. Letters and contracts are more potent weapons than pistols and rifles."

"Tell that to someone who just got shot," Wedge said.

Dumay dismissed the grim killer with an impatient wave of his hand and turned to his spy. "Wyatt, you had better get back before someone starts to wonder where you've gone. Mr. Wedge, get our people ready. We're riding north. We'll combine forces with the miners up there and make our big push. I am ready to call Heck Martin's bluff."

CHAPTER 10

Dumay rode beside Wedge on the buckboard of the lead wagon, like Caesar at the front of his army.

His longstanding irritation had finally passed, swept away by the exciting moment and impending victory.

He couldn't wait to see the look on Heck Martin's face when the mountain man saw the size of Dumay's force.

They made quite a racket marching alongside the string of mining wagons. They shouted and laughed and pounded their chests and shook their rifles overhead.

They were excited, too. And while Dumay found their shouting distasteful, he understood it well enough.

These men were street toughs and sailors and vagabonds with bad attitudes. They had marched here all the way from San Francisco for this exact moment, when, by show of force, they would crush the resolve of Heck Martin and his people.

Beside Dumay, Wedge looked anything but excited. He

maintained a slow pace and scanned the surrounding valley with narrowed eyes.

That was fine. It was his job to protect Dumay, after all, not join in celebration.

Wedge's head stopped turning, and his eyes narrowed further, studying a specific spot on one slope. "Ready now," he whispered.

Dumay felt a prickle of fear. "What do you mean?"

"Gunman up there in those trees."

"Heck Martin?"

"Don't know. Just saw a glint of steel, there and gone."

"Just a glint? Well, that could have been anything."

"There's another," Wedge said.

Behind them, amidst the long train of wagons, oblivious men carried on shouting and laughing.

"If someone shoots, you get down in the wagon behind me and make yourself small," Wedge said. "That's why I chose this wagon for you. It has the thickest sidewalls."

Dumay felt another prickle of fear. "They wouldn't dare to shoot at us. We have too many men."

"You keep telling yourself that, Mr. Dumay, but I'd still recommend getting down in the wagon if you're wrong."

As they rolled down the road, Wedge spotted additional men in the forest above them. There was no shooting, but a heavy tension held over the morning—a much heavier tension, Dumay had to admit, than anything he would have expected.

He was a man used to paving his own way and entering into conflicts with certain guarantees in place—something he had, in all fairness, gone to great effort and expense to do here as well—and it irritated him to realize he was not in total control of this situation because these people refused to understand what they were up against.

Then, spotting none other than Heck Martin standing in the road ahead, blocking their way, Dumay smiled.

Now it was time to *make* these ignorant fools understand.

Martin held his ground, standing there with a rifle in his hands and a stony expression on his face. Dumay had to admit the young man looked formidable. Part of it was his size. He was very tall and muscular with broad shoulders.

But this wasn't a boxing match, and Martin's great size would only make him a larger target for the many bullets that would fly in his direction if Dumay gave the command to fire.

Not that Dumay wanted that, of course. Unlike some men, Dumay was able to look beyond any single conflict and do his best not only to win but also arrange the aftermath in his favor.

Not that he would be looking for any kind of reconciliation with Martin, of course. Far from it. The main reason he had come all this way was to destroy the man now standing before him, blocking his path.

But he did not wish to destroy him with bullets. He wished to destroy his little kingdom, the faith others had in him, and his faith in himself.

He wished to ruin Heck Martin financially and psychologically, to leave him stunned and regretful.

That, more than anything else.

Heck Martin must deeply regret the day he crossed Percival Dumay.

For the moment, however, Heck Martin's hard features showed nothing like regret or uncertainty, even though he clearly saw the massive column of raucous men walking his way.

Martin stood alone at the very edge of town.

No, not alone, Dumay realized.

Because on both sides of the road, men peered around the sides of shops and cabins. Dumay saw the dark lines of rifle barrels jutting out from each figure.

Still, they were not many.

Further on, numerous figures watched from atop the walls of the picket fence surrounding Fort Seeker.

Were those women?

Yes, they were, Dumay realized. But they, too, held rifles.

And some of them, he realized with a chill, were pointing their rifles in his direction.

That certainly wasn't very ladylike. What was wrong with these people?

Drawing to within thirty feet of Heck Martin, Wedge started to slow the wagon.

"No," Dumay said. "Drive the oxen right up to him. Make him take a step back."

CHAPTER 11

"Y ou sure you want to push like that, boss?"

"I'm sure. Now do it."

Wedge looked at him for a second but said nothing.

Was that a flicker of irritation in Wedge's eyes?

Perhaps. The sooner Dumay was rid of this killer, the better.

But for now, Wedge was very much necessary. If Heck Martin really was as stubborn as he now looked and turned out to be stupid enough to try something, Wedge would gun him down as he had so many others.

And when dealing with the likes of Heck Martin, that was a very nice guarantee to have.

Dumay's irritation and dismay washed away again as a wave of triumph crashed over him. This was it, the moment he'd been engineering for over a year, the reason he had given up his comfortable life, spent a great deal of money, and traveled across the wilderness.

He was about to break Heck Martin—not to mention the

dreams of all these small-minded sodbusters. Then, Dumay would spend the rest of his life savoring this moment.

Dumay felt a surge of excitement as they drew closer.

Heck Martin stood his ground.

Twenty feet.

Ten.

Heck Martin raised a hand. Not the one holding the rifle. The empty hand, its fingers splayed, directed not at Dumay or Wedge but the oxen.

The wagon stopped.

"I told you not to stop," Dumay whispered with irritation.

"I didn't," Wedge said, staring at Heck Marin, whose outstretched hand paused a second longer, mere inches from the skull of the mesmerized oxen. "The animals did."

"Time is up," Dumay announced loudly. "Move aside, Mr. Martin. We are coming through."

"I'm not going anywhere," Heck Martin said.

Dumay flashed with anger. What an imbecile, trying to stand in the way of an army!

As if to illustrate this point, dozens of Dumay's men moved forward on either side of the wagon and loomed at the ready, sneering and laughing.

One word, Dumay realized, and they would charge forward and pummel Heck Martin into the mud with their clubs, rifle butts, fists, and boots.

"You must move," Dumay said. "I am bringing men and equipment through."

Heck Martin shook his head. "Road's closed."

"You're going to break the law, then?" Dumay said. "You're going to stop me from exercising my rights?"

Dumay had expected Heck Martin to either step aside or lose his temper. Strangely, Martin did neither. He remained simply resolute.

"You're the one who's breaking the law, Dumay. You're trespassing."

"If you read the affidavit, you'll know that isn't true. Because I own these mineral rights, the judge granted me a right of way anywhere in this valley that I deemed necessary to the extraction of resources. And I deem it necessary for you to get out of my way so we can move past."

Dumay smiled with satisfaction and sat back.

Heck Martin said nothing for a long moment. The wind ruffled his black hair. He looked up at the hills then shifted his blue-eyed gaze to the opposite slope.

Dumay felt a stab of impatience. It was frustrating, waiting for Martin, and he didn't appreciate being ignored.

When Dumay spoke again, it was out of this irritation. "Get out of the way, man, or—"

He cut off, almost issuing an unwise threat.

"Or what?" Heck Martin said.

Beside Dumay, Wedge shifted.

Dumay understood that things had changed. Suddenly, everything hung in the balance. One false move, one wrong word, everything here could erupt cataclysmically.

He had to use logic now, had to stick to the plan. He couldn't allow emotion to trick him into doing or saying something brash.

This situation, this valley, it was all his for the taking. He had made certain of that well before leaving California—or at least, he had paved the way to take it before anyone back there started asking hard questions.

The one way to mess that up now would be doing something stupid, something impulsive.

"Don't try to confuse the issue," Dumay said quickly. "Do you confess? Are you trying to block a court-mandated right-of-way? Are you trying to keep a man from his lawful property?"

"Lawful property?" Heck Martin said, and his expression changed at last—not, as Dumay had expected, by twisting with frustration, but rather with a wolfish smile. "This land was discovered and claimed by a man named Badger Yates. His son, Seeker, was born and raised here and now owns the valley, along with my wife and me. We bought it legally, hold the title, and improved this ground, building a fort, a trading post, a town, and the road you seem to misconstrue as public property."

"The affidavit-"

"Furthermore," Heck Martin interrupted, making Dumay choke with fury, "we brought a large herd of cattle into this valley, and these cattle help to supply both the soldiers at Fort Laramie and emigrants passing on the trail, the very folks this nation is counting on to make the Westward expansion a reality. This is my land, Dumay, and my road, and I'm not budging."

"Are you blind, man? Or just stupid?" Dumay snapped. Even as the words left his mouth, he knew he was going off script, but Heck Martin was so infuriating, he couldn't help himself. "Look right in front of your eyes. Look at these men. Look at their number. Look at their clubs and rifles. You don't stand a chance. Why, one word from me, and these men will plow over you, trample you into the mud, smash through your picket fence, and take what they want."

Heck Martin's expression didn't change in the least. Again, he took his time before responding, stoking the fires of frustration within Dumay.

When Heck Martin finally did speak, the wolfish grin returned to his face. "You left out one part. If you give that word, before any of your thugs even lays a hand on me, you're a dead man. You got no fewer than four dozen rifles trained on you right now. On *you*, Dumay. They'd be shooting from all angles. And make no mistake about it. These folks, they're not toting rifles for show. They're hunters, and they've faced men before. I'm guessing most of them would hit their mark."

Suddenly, Dumay was cold. Very, very cold.

He knew Martin was speaking the truth. Somehow, he had never considered this possibility.

Yes, Wedge had cautioned against his riding in front, but Dumay had felt safe, given his legal armor and the strength of his army, and he had wanted to give Heck Martin the news and wanted a front row seat when Martin fell apart.

But Heck Martin hadn't fallen apart. He'd stood his ground.

And now Dumay knew without a shred of doubt that he, himself, stood directly upon death's doorstep. One wrong word, one unwise action, and he would be very, very dead.

And not just one word or action from him…

To either side of him, his rowdy thugs tensed like so many vicious hounds, straining to come off their leads. If one of them, just one, jumped forward…

Dumay gave an involuntary shudder.

Heck Martin's grin widened, looking more wolfish than ever.

"You'll... pay... for... this," Dumay promised, biting off each word carefully.

Martin said nothing.

"Turn around!" Dumay shouted to his men. "We're heading back to camp."

The men grumbled yet complied, and Dumay sat, burning with humiliation and rage as Wedge began the painstakingly slow process of turning the oxen back in the other direction.

That rage and humiliation burned all the hotter as they finally started rolling northward, and a boy's voice cackled triumphantly, "Look at 'em run, Heck! You plucked old Dumay like a prairie hen!"

CHAPTER 12

As Dumay's forces went around the bend and out of sight, men came from behind the shops and cabins displaying expressions ranging from pale-faced fear to giddy excitement.

Paul Wolfe exhibited both extremes. As color returned to his face, a tough smile joined it. Heck knew the twelve-year-old grew nervous at times like these, but he'd stood his ground more than once.

That's what matters, of course. Tough men don't stand because they're not afraid. Tough men stand when they're afraid.

And the widow's son might be small and skinny, but he was well on his way to becoming a tough man. In fact, he already had the tough part down. Now, he just had to become a man.

And since a big part of being a man is talking to other men as a man, Heck called the boy forward. "Paul, run on up the trail. Tell everyone to stay in position a while longer just in case Dumay has a change of heart."

"Yes, sir," Paul said, and set off.

The others gathered around Heck.

"Good job, men," Heck told them. "We stood our ground. Dumay didn't expect that."

"He looked funny at the end," Seeker laughed. "Looked like somebody ate the chicken and left him with the gizzards!"

"This is no laughing matter, young Master Yates," said the schoolmaster, Titus Haines. A former cavalry officer, Titus didn't look afraid, but he certainly looked concerned. "A force that size would have smashed us."

"We had them covered from all sides," A.J. Blum blustered, gripping his double-barrel 10-gauge shotgun in both hands.

"Yeah, there really were a lot of them, though," Doc said.

The Pillsbury Brothers nodded in agreement. Both of the farmers looked half sick with fear. Beside them, fourteen-year-old Franky seemed to be faring slightly better than his father and uncle.

"Well, it doesn't matter now," Abe Zale crowed. "Dumay made his play, and Heck called his bluff. They're gone."

"Gone for now," Doc said. "But they'll be back. You heard Dumay. This is war now."

"It ain't gonna be a war," Maguire said. "Not yet anyway. Dumay doesn't want war. He's got a reputation to think of."

Heck nodded. "And we don't want war, either. There are too many of them. If we fought smart, outflanked them, and found ways to attack, we might beat them... but at what cost?"

"We would take heavy losses," Doc said. "Even if we beat them, we wouldn't win a war."

The gate to the fort had opened, and some of the folks—a

few women, including Hope, but mostly men—were rushing out to hear what happened.

In these men, Heck had detected reluctance or paralyzing fear. That's why he'd stationed them inside the fort. Fighting against superior numbers, he couldn't afford to have front-line defenders break ranks and infect the others with panic.

At the head of this group was Wyatt Henley, who rushed headlong into the circle of defenders and congratulated Heck on making Dumay back down. But even as Wyatt offered congratulations, he set to spreading fear again. "I don't know why they turned away. There were so many of them. And Dumay's men looked tough as nails!"

Wyatt glanced around for confirmation and gained a few nods.

"Those boys in front looked ready to rumble," Maguire said, "but I don't think this Dumay character has any idea of what he's doing. He might be a gold baron or whatever, but I don't think he knows the first thing about mixing it up. And as far as his men go, I think he put the mean ones in front to make an impression. I've bumped into some of the cowpokes down in the lower valleys, you know, when our cattle strayed toward theirs. They were all right. Just seemed like a bunch of run-of-the-mill punchers to me. I think this Dumay is mostly bluster."

"I don't think so," Burt Bickle said. "Man like that, a man who's built up big businesses like he has, well he's got to be driven. And you could see how angry he was."

"Yeah, but he still backed off."

"Saw all those barrels, did the math, and didn't like the answer he got," A.J. Plum chuckled. "He knows he'd lose a lot of men."

"He doesn't care about his men," Heck said. "That's not why he pulled out. He cares about himself. That was the only reason he turned around. I told him if he did anything to me, you boys would blow him off that wagon."

"I sure would've," Seeker said.

"Well," Doc said, "if Dumay only cares about his own safety, what's to stop him, now that he's out of harm's way, from sending his thugs back down the road at us now?"

Everyone shifted their eyes northward, but no one came screaming at them.

"Good point, Doc," Heck said. "We're gonna have to keep a close watch and stay ready. I think Dusty's right. I think Dumay cares too much about his reputation to pull something that brazen, but I could be wrong, so I sure wouldn't go betting our lives on that assumption."

"We should hit them while they're on the run," Seeker said.

"They're too big of a force for us to try that," Titus said. "We're not a bunch of nomadic raiders, after all. They would just come charging back."

"I don't mean attack the men," Seeker said. "I mean ride south, stampede their cattle, and burn their cabins and wagons, all their supplies. See how long they last with no food and no shelter."

"A barbaric plan," Titus said regarding the boy soberly, "but not without merit."

"You do make a good point, little brother," Heck said, "and you're thinking the right way. If this stretches out, we're gonna have to break them. But a move like that, right now? It would force Dumay's hand. He'd call for an all-out attack, and we can't afford that."

"We could weather the storm," Seeker said. "Half of us could hole up in the fort. The other half could run the ridges with plenty of shot and powder, shooting down on them."

"Again, little brother, your ideas might work. But the timing is wrong. Let's sit back and see how Dumay reacts. We might find that, despite all his tough talk, he doesn't have the stomach for a real fight. Most men don't, not when it comes down to it."

Of course, even as Heck said this, he knew at least one of Dumay's men had plenty of fight in him. Frank Wedge. Through the whole engagement, Wedge had sat there, relaxed but ready.

Eventually, Heck's gut told him, regardless of Dumay's resolve, Heck and Wedge were going to end up settling their differences like men, and one or both of them was going to end up dead.

CHAPTER 13

Dumay paced.

He had never been so insulted, so humiliated, in all his life.

Heck Martin had made him look like a fool!

Apparently, the other two men in the room, Jem Pulcher and Trace Boon, had detected his anger, because they sat meekly at the table, watching him with nervous eyes.

"Why didn't Wyatt tell me what Heck Martin was planning?" Dumay demanded. "Why didn't he tell me the slopes would be full of snipers?"

"Heck probably didn't even tell him," Trace Boon said. "Remember? Wyatt said something like that last time he was here. Said Heck wouldn't tell them anything beforehand."

"Sounds like Heck," Jem Pulcher said, shaking his head. "Always gotta boss everybody around. He thinks he's a big wheel."

"That's what a man of action does when he's surrounded by

idiots," Dumay snapped. He was coming to loathe these men, especially the detestable Pulcher. "Where's my food? It's well past supper time."

"I'm guessing your chef is still putting it together," Trace said.

"I know that, you fool!" Dumay shouted.

The long, slow retreat had taken forever, as had ironing out the confusion of the men. Finally, he had come back here to his valley headquarters, leaving perhaps a third of his men to guard the mining equipment, which was too heavy to transport without an established trail.

Now, it was well after dark, and he was hungry and angry and didn't know what to do.

Nothing had gone as planned. Heck Martin had refused to budge, completely disregarded the affidavit, and hadn't even seemed to notice the size of Dumay's force.

Through it all, Martin had remained maddeningly imperturbable.

"Should've just run him over," Jem said. "That would've fixed him."

"If I had, then his friends would have shot me—and you'd be stuck in the wilderness with no employer."

"I'm just saying that's what he deserved, getting trampled by oxen and runned over by a wagon."

"The audacity of the man," Dumay said, and he experienced another chill as he remembered Martin explaining about the snipers. "What sort of man makes a threat like that?"

"Heck's a hard man," Trace said.

"He's got no scruples," Jem said. "That's his problem. He's not like us, Mr. Dumay. He's a savage."

Dumay nodded. "You're right for once. He's a barbarian with no respect for the law or common decency."

Jem and Trace sat there nodding like a couple of idiots.

"Yup," Jem said. "It's terrible."

"Well, if Heck Martin wants a fight, he'll have it," Dumay said, and stopped pacing to pound the table with his fist.

"That's the spirit, sir," Jem laughed.

"What are you fixing to do, Mr. Dumay?" Trace asked nervously.

"It is time to strike." Dumay lifted his chin slightly. "Go fetch Mr. Wedge."

CHAPTER 14

Several miles north of Dumay, Heck Martin was also pacing back and forth. Only instead of conversing with a pair of traitorous, self-serving cowards, he was talking to his intelligent, beloved wife, Hope, while their boy slept a short distance away in his crib.

"What do you think he's going to do, Heck?" Hope asked.

Heck shook his head. "No way to know. Just have to wait. Watch and wait, that is. Tomorrow, before first light, I'm gonna ride down the ridge and see what I can see. I'll send Seeker in the opposite direction."

"You think they'll attack?"

"They might. We have to be ready for it."

Hope nodded grimly. "We're as ready as can be. But do you really think they will?"

"I don't know. Not right away. I don't think they'll come right at us. If they were gonna do that, they already would've as soon as Dumay was safe."

"You think he's got something else up his sleeve?"

"I do."

"Like what?"

Heck shrugged. "That's what's bothering me. I got no idea. I think we surprised him today. He rolled in here, expecting us to surrender, but we stood strong. You should've seen him when I spelled out what would happen if he tried to do something to me."

Hope grinned. "Scared?"

"He shuddered."

She laughed.

"Thing is, though, he's still confident," Heck said. "You could hear it in his voice when he threatened me at the end. He was embarrassed and mad, but he still thinks he's got us."

"But again, if that's the case, why didn't he just get to safety and send his men back?"

"I don't think he wants that any more than we do. Not because he cares about his men. He doesn't care about them. He cares about himself and his reputation. He blundered today, but he's no dummy. He's a hard driver who's used to winning. I don't know how he messed with our title or got that affidavit, but the fact he did shows how powerful he is."

Hope shook her head. "I hate corruption. Why do people stand for it?"

"I don't know. Corruption repels me. I've never associated with cheats or thieves, so I don't know how they think."

"Which makes you vulnerable to their dirty tricks."

Heck nodded. "Dumay knows so little about fighting he walked straight into a situation where he'd be the first one to die. He thought he could intimidate us. He should've understood that he'd backed us into a corner where he was giving us no choice but to kill him. So in that way, he's pretty stupid. And he knew that in the end. But he was still confident."

"Meaning he has something else," Hope said, "some other weapon."

"Right. He must've gone to a lot of trouble and spent a lot of money to do all that with the title and affidavit. I'm guessing if he went to that much trouble, he probably went even further. Question is, what else does he have planned? What's the next stage of his attack?"

CHAPTER 15

When Wedge arrived, Dumay kicked out Jem and Trace. Those two idiots lacked character.

Wedge, on the other hand, was character in a black suit with a hat to match. The man wasn't much of a conversationalist and even grated on Dumay at times, but Wedge knew fighting, knew death, and knew how to command the respect of the loud thugs who now gathered around campfires outside, clamoring for food.

"You wished to see me, Mr. Dumay?" Wedge said as the door closed behind the retreating miners.

"Yes. I need you to do something for me. Something very important."

"Want me to go back up there, call out Heck Martin, and finish this?"

"You mean kill him?" Dumay said, shock plain in his voice.

Wedge spread his hands. "It's why you hired me."

"I hired you as my bodyguard, not as an assassin."

"I'm not sure there will end up being a difference, once we get down to it."

"What do you mean, Mr. Wedge?"

"This Heck Martin, he's not going to quit until he's dead."

Dumay rolled his eyes. "You don't really believe that."

Wedge just stared at Dumay for a long second. The straight line of his mouth hardened, and his pale blue eyes glittered dangerously.

Dumay squirmed beneath that menacing gaze. It was like being face-to-face with a poisonous serpent.

Apparently, either by rolling his eyes or expressing doubt in what Wedge had said, he'd managed to offend the killer. He must remember to be more careful. Despite the man's polished shoes and neatly tailored black suit, he was in many ways as primitive as a caveman.

Was he supposed to offer some sort of apology, or would that only make Wedge angrier?

Before Dumay could come to a decision on the matter, Wedge spoke again.

"I assumed he'd stand just based on our first interaction and the various stories I've heard about him. But after today, I'm certain. He would sooner die than budge."

"You can't," Dumay started and caught himself. "I disagree. Heck Martin has too much to lose. A wife, a child, a fortune…"

"And none of it's worth a penny if he has to surrender his manhood to save it."

"Why would you say that?"

"Because it's true. Men like us live by a code."

"Men like you? Are you telling me you relate to this yokel?"

"Yes, I do. At least in the way it matters. And yokel doesn't come into it. I'm not talking about where he's from or how he talks or any of that. For some men, there's one thing more important than love or money or even life itself."

"And what, precisely, is that?"

Wedge leaned back against the wall beside the door and looked thoughtful for a moment. "I suppose you could call it the truth."

"I had no idea you were such a philosopher, Mr. Wedge."

"You kill as many people as I have—or as Heck Martin has, for that matter—you must choose to become either a beast or a philosopher."

Dumay managed not to roll his eyes. Instead, he humored the killer, who for some reason was trying to impress him with all this nonsense. "And why did you choose to become a philosopher rather than a beast?"

Wedge smiled slightly. "Philosophers live longer."

"Well, if I'm honest, I have no idea what you're talking about. Heck Martin has much to lose here, and whatever you mean by truth, it can't come close to a wife, child, and money."

"Those things won't ever be loaded on a scale," Wedge said, "unless they already were, a long time ago, when Heck Martin was made."

"And when you were made, I suppose?"

Wedge gave a little nod. "Men like us, we are perfectly capable of standing up to moments that would terrify other men, but we are at the same time incapable of living a lie. If Heck Martin ran off with all those things, he wouldn't even be Heck Martin anymore. He would be a runner, a coward, a house divided. And he knows that in his bones. That's why he'll never back down. The only way to win this valley is to kill him."

"No," Dumay said. He didn't care about Wedge's insane philosophical ramblings, but he very much cared about the man's conclusion. "I'm not a murderer. Besides, I don't want him dead, I want him destitute. I want to ruin his life, not end it. If it's over, he can't ponder the error of his ways and regret having crossed me. That's what I want from him, not death, regret, soul-devouring regret."

Wedge arched a brow, looking at Dumay with utter puzzlement.

Dumay said, "We need to escalate things with Mr. Martin, but we need to refrain from triggering an all-out war. We just need to nudge him, get him to do something he shouldn't. And that will give me the leverage I need to crush him."

"How is that, boss?"

"I'll tell you when I'm ready. For now, I want you to go speak with some of the men."

"Which ones?"

"The cattlemen for starters. And I want you to handpick a few of the toughest, meanest fighters."

"You mean fist fighters? I don't know that there's a gunman in the whole bunch."

"Yes, fist fighters. Strong men who don't mind inflicting pain. In fact, find some who like to inflict it."

CHAPTER 16

Some mornings, the first time you set eyes on a calf, you know he's determined to cause trouble that day.

It was a thing Dusty Maguire knew from his years of working cattle, a thing he'd witnessed countless times.

This morning, a red-speckled calf stood a bit off from the others, staring at Maguire from the get-go. The morning was cool for this time of year, and spirals of steam twisted up from the cow patties to where the steer stared at Maguire and chewed his cud, managing to look simultaneously insolent and mischievous.

Which to someone who didn't know cattle might sound ludicrous. But Maguire did know cattle. Knew them a lot better than he knew people. And he knew this steer was fixing to get into mischief today.

And sure enough, when Maguire and the other cowpokes pushed the herd south into the tall grass of the valley between Heck's land and Dumay's, the red-speckled calf kept on going.

Maguire was riding the southern perimeter of the herd when he saw the calf stray off and disappear around the bend.

Which was also the point Heck had told them not to cross. None of this was Heck's grass other than by virtue of having grazed it for several months. But the herd needed it now, having already depleted the forage north of here.

But going further south was inviting trouble with Dumay.

Not that Maguire expected any trouble with Dumay's punchers. They seemed all right, and he'd ride with most of them. In fact, he'd rather ride with them than his current partner, Wyatt, any day.

Wyatt was all right. You told him to do something, he'd do it. But he would never be a top hand. He was more of an all-purpose ranch hand than a cowboy.

Nothing wrong with that, of course, but a cowboy likes to work with other cowboys—and besides, Wyatt talked too much. He was always asking questions, prying into folks' business, and it rubbed Maguire the wrong way.

But Heck insisted no one south of the boundary ride alone, so they each had a partner, and today, Wyatt was Maguire's.

"Come on," Maguire called to Wyatt. "That ornery calf just disappeared around the corner."

"What ornery calf?" Wyatt said.

Maguire spat, disgusted by Wyatt's lack of awareness. "Doesn't matter. Let's go round him up."

"All right," Wyatt said. "Stupid calf. How come he ran off like that?"

Maguire didn't bother to answer. He spurred his horse and chased after the calf.

Coming around the corner, he reined in, almost colliding with another rider.

Several of Dumay's men had pushed right up to the bend. Behind them, Dumay's small herd grazed.

The calf was straining against the rope one of Dumay's punchers had lassoed it with.

"Howdy," Maguire said with a friendly smile to the closest man. "You boys are ranging farther north today. Almost crashed into you."

The man said nothing and did not return Maguire's smile. He leaned and spat, then gave Maguire a hard look.

That's when Maguire realized this man was a stranger. He'd never seen him among Dumay's punchers. He sat his horse all right but didn't really look like a cowboy. With his hard eyes, thick build, and the long scar running down one side of his face, the man looked more like a barroom brawler than a cowpoke.

Maguire glanced at the rest of the men and realized most of them were unfamiliar, too. "Morning, fellas."

They said nothing. The new boys, who all looked rough, stared at him.

The few he'd seen before looked away, refusing to make eye contact.

Now just what was going on here?

Maguire felt a chill and had to fight the urge to pull his six-shooter. Doing so might be misconstrued, of course, exactly the type of blunder that could lead to real trouble.

So what if these boys were less than friendly? It didn't mean he had to go filling his hand with iron.

Hopefully, Wyatt had the sense to show similar restraint. Wyatt seemed a little jumpy sometimes.

He turned to check but saw no sign of Wyatt.

Where was he?

"You're trespassing," the closest man said.

"Just running down that ornery calf," Maguire said, offering another smile.

"What calf?" the man said then turned to the tough-looking punchers, who were riding over to join them. "You boys see a calf?"

"We didn't see no calf," one man said, riding past Maguire.

Maguire turned his horse, not wanting the man behind him, but another of the men cut around him to the other side.

What were these boys doing? Where was Wyatt?

He didn't like this. Not one bit. He had to get the calf and get back to the herd.

"That calf right there," Maguire said, pointing to the ornery calf trying to dig in his hooves as the cowboy who'd roped him started heading southward, away from his mother—and toward Dumay's herd. "Hey now, don't you take that calf off that way. That's our calf, not yours."

Indignation leapt up in Maguire, temporarily overshadowing his unease. Every cowboy hates a rustler, and these men were trying to take that calf.

"That's our calf," the man with the scar said, easing his horse forward so it was shoulder to shoulder with Maguire's horse.

"Oh no, he ain't," Maguire said. "That's our calf, and you know it."

The man glared at him. "You calling me a liar, mister?"

"If you're trying to steal our calf, yes, I am." Then Maguire lifted his voice, calling after the thief who really was taking the calf away. "Hey! You bring him—"

His head jerked sharply, exploding in a spray of stars and pain.

Maguire was already falling, knocked from the saddle, when he realized he'd been sucker punched. Then he hit the ground awkwardly, and fresh pain—bad pain this time, worse than the punch, the pain of a serious shoulder injury—knocked all thoughts from his head.

He groaned and spat dirt from his mouth, tasting blood, and tried to push up off the ground, but his left arm wouldn't work, so he rolled to the other side and sat up. "Why did you—"

Again, his words were cut off, this time by a blow from behind. Not a fist but a boot to the ribs.

The kick knocked him over and filled him with pain.

Maguire felt like laying there until the pain passed, but he was a scrapper and knew the only way out of this was to fight. So he kept rolling and got to his feet and reached for his pistol.

They rushed him before he could get it free. Four of five of them. Maguire wasn't sure. He just saw the guy with the scar coming straight at him with a fist drawn back and the blur of motion coming from all other directions.

Maguire dipped his head, and the punch merely grazed him, but in the same instant, men grabbed his arms and yanked, and someone punched him hard in the kidney.

He cried out, both from the blow to the back and the excruciating pain in his injured arm, which someone was now yanking behind him and pinning there.

His gun fell free and one of Dumay's punchers picked it up.

Where was Wyatt?

Desperate, unable to break free, Maguire called, "Wyatt!"

Before he could call again, the scarred man slapped him hard across the face.

"You're trespassing on Mr. Dumay's land," the scarred man said, his dark eyes gleaming with malice.

Maguire spat blood. "Bunch of no-good rustlers. You think you're tough, why don't you fight me alone?"

The man grinned nastily and tilted his head, eyeing Maguire's busted arm. "Your arm don't look so hot, buddy. I'm no doc, but it looks busted to me. Does this hurt?"

He hauled off and swatted Maguire in the damaged arm.

Maguire screamed and nearly passed out from the pain.

He stumbled forward and realized they had let him go.

"You tell Heck Martin things have changed," the scarred man said. "You cross us, this is what you get. Come on, boys. Let him have it."

Knowing what was about to happen, Maguire lashed out with a quick right that smashed into the man's eye, making him wince and curse.

And then they were on him.

CHAPTER 17

Hodges prodded at his sore eye as the other men lashed the semi-conscious cowboy to his horse.

His eye was tender, and the one corner was swollen so it made his vision a little funny, which was annoying.

It made him feel like punching the cowboy a few more times. But that might kill him, and Wedge had been clear about that.

Don't kill anybody, Wedge had told them. *You kill anybody, I'm going to hold you accountable.*

And the last thing Hodges wanted was Wedge holding him accountable for anything.

So he walked over and patted the bloodied puncher on the leg. "You hold on tight, buddy. You fall off there, you're gonna die."

The man groaned incoherently.

Hodges laughed and slapped the horse on the rump. "Go

home," he snapped, and the horse trotted off to the north, the battered cowhand clinging to its neck.

Hodges laughed, watching him go.

Then he realized the other men with him weren't laughing. In fact, they looked worried.

Which surprised Hodges. After all, they weren't cowardly cowpokes. He'd already sent them off with the calf. Every last one of these men was from the docks. They'd all been in brawls and done rough work.

But now, they sure didn't look tough. Especially Tom. He looked like he'd been kicked in the stomach.

"What's wrong with you?" Hodges demanded.

"We went too far," Tom said. "I think maybe we crossed a line."

"Crossed a line?" Hodges said. "He's the one crossed the line, and we let him have it."

Ben Gunn spoke up. "Tom's right. Everything's changed. I can feel it."

The other two nodded.

Hodges felt a stab of annoyance. "What's gotten into you? You sound like a bunch of frightened little girls."

Tom cast a wary look northward, where the valley twisted and closed off their view. "That tall fella, he don't seem the type to sit around waiting for apologies."

"I was thinking the same thing," Schmidt said. He was just a kid, but up until now, he'd always had plenty of sand. "Maybe we ought to get out of here before it's too late."

Hodges was shocked to see the others nodding.

"What in the world are you talking about?" he blustered. "Sound like a bunch of cowards."

Tom shuddered. "I'm telling you, Hodges. Everything's changed. That tall fella—"

"I hope you're right," Hodges snarled irritably. "I hope Heck Martin comes riding down here to set things right. There are five of us, aren't there? We'll stomp him toothless."

"What if he doesn't want to fight that way?" Tom said.

"Yeah," Schmidt said. "What if he pulls his gun?"

"We got guns, too, don't we?" Hodges said.

"Yeah, but I never—"

"You just point it and pull the trigger," Hodges snapped. "Besides, why would he? We didn't shoot his buddy. If he wants to start shooting, Wedge will take care of him."

On that point, no one disagreed.

Then that rat Wyatt Henley came riding out of the hillside brush at the edge of the field. "You boys sure did a number on him, didn't you?"

"That's right," Hodges said. He couldn't stand Wyatt. He was the type that would roll over to the cops for a wooden nickel. "We did exactly what Mr. Wedge told us to do. That'll rattle their cages."

"Anybody asks," Wyatt said, "you haven't seen me.

With that, the scoundrel rode off toward the north, where he would no doubt pretend that he'd missed the whole scrap.

"Somebody ought to put a bullet between his eyes," Hodges grumbled, and again, no one disagreed.

"What do we do now?" Tom asked.

Hodges thought for a minute. "Ride back and tell Wedge what happened. I don't trust them cowboys to do it. They might cut and run for California."

The other men shared a look.

What did that mean? Were they really thinking of bailing on Dumay?

"What do we do?" Schmidt asked as Tom rode off.

"You stand right here with me. We're gonna see what they do."

CHAPTER 18

Heck, Seeker, Paul Wolfe, and Abe Zale sat their horses atop the northern ridge, staring down at the thirty-some men stationed at Dumay's upper camp.

Even as Heck was panning his spyglasses back and forth over these men and their squalor, his thoughts were tugged southward. For some reason, it felt like he should be at the end of things, not here.

"Why are they there?" Paul asked.

"Why do you think, Paul?" Heck asked. The boy had come a long way and talked now with growing confidence among men, so Heck wasn't going to baby him.

Paul lifted his mother's spyglasses and studied the men for a while before responding. The binoculars were a good set, which fit what Heck knew of the Widow, who clearly valued quality over quantity.

"I guess they're guarding the wagons," Paul said, "since they can't drag all that heavy equipment to the other camp without a road."

"I reckon you're right," Heck said. "It's another reason to never surrender the road. Keeping them apart weakens them and complicates things for Dumay."

Paul nodded.

"They're pretty rowdy," Abe said.

"Yeah," Seeker agreed. "Way rowdier than the other camp."

"Good," Heck said, and the question of the southern camp still nagged at him. "The longer we can stall them, the better. Men like this get bored and start messing with each other."

"I hope they get in a big ol' fight and kill each other," Seeker declared.

"That sure would be convenient, little brother." The idea of the southern camp was still bothering him, so Heck put away his spyglasses. As a mountain man, you learned to pay attention to your hunches, and this one kept nagging at him.

"Seeker, Abe, stick around and keep an eye on these men. I want to know if they try anything, and keep an eye out for wagon trains. We haven't had any business down there since these boys showed up. It's late in the season, but we would usually still be getting some stragglers. My guess is Dumay is driving folks away. Paul, come with me. We'll go see what's happening down the line."

Heck and Paul rode across the ridge, heading south and nearing the southern valleys, when Heck saw what he first thought was a riderless horse trotting slowly north at the edge of the big herd.

"Hold on," he told Paul and stopped Red and pulled out his spyglasses and took a closer look.

There was a rider. Seeing the horse, he assumed it was Maguire. He was laid out over the horse, clutching its neck.

Which suggested he was hurt.

Where was his partner, Wyatt?

Feeling a wave of foreboding, Heck rode downhill, followed by Paul.

Heck didn't wait for the boy. He charged straight across the field, scanning as he went for any sign of Wyatt or any threats.

Just as he reached Maguire, the cowboy groaned, slipped from the saddle, and tumbled off the horse.

Heck barely managed to catch him and thanked God he'd been able to reach him in time. Otherwise, Maguire might've broken his neck.

The cowboy was a mess.

And not from falling off his horse.

Someone had clearly beaten the good-natured cowboy. Severely and cruelly.

Maguire's eyes were swollen shut. His nose was broken. His lips were split in a dozen places, and his normally easy smile was missing teeth.

A volcano of rage erupted in Heck. He was normally good at controlling his emotions, but his blood boiled at the sight of Maguire, who always had a kind word for everyone, even Dumay's drovers.

"What happened?" Paul said, riding up, his face ghostly pale.

"Somebody thrashed him," Heck said.

Maguire struggled back to consciousness and tried to open his swollen eyes. "Heck?"

"It's me, Dusty. I'm here with you now."

"They beat me, Heck."

"Who?"

"Dumay's men. Five of them. Never saw them before." He panted with weakness, clutching his midsection. "Hurt me bad, Heck. Took your calf. Tried to stop them, but—"

With a terrible groan, Maguire lost consciousness.

"Is he okay, Heck?" Paul asked.

"I don't know," Heck answered truthfully. "They hurt him pretty bad."

"Where's his partner?"

Heck frowned. "I don't know. He was paired off with Wyatt today."

Heck's mind raced, considering possibilities, none of which were good. Most ended with Wyatt somewhere on the ground in Maguire's back trail.

Paul looked to the south. "I don't see him anywhere."

"Neither do I, Paul. I gotta find him. He's one of ours. I won't leave him."

Paul was clearly frightened, but he nodded. "All right, Heck. Let's go, then."

"No, you gotta get Maguire to Doc and Hope. He needs their help." Heck lifted Maguire onto his horse and lashed him safely in place as quickly as he could. "You ride close and don't let him fall, you hear?"

"Yes, sir."

"Good man. You ride up a little way, you should bump into Ray and Zeke. They'll help you get him back."

"Ride with me, Heck," Paul pleaded.

"You can handle this, Paul."

"That's not what I mean. Ride with me. Ray and Zeke can take Mr. Maguire back. Then I'll ride with you and go find

Wyatt. I don't want you riding alone into trouble."

Heck appreciated the boy's bravery but shook his head. "I gotta go now in case they hurt Wyatt bad. It could mean the difference between life and death. Wyatt's one of ours. I won't let him lay there."

And with that, Heck yanked the Colt from his belt and rode south as fast as he could travel.

CHAPTER 19

Dumay was feeling quite good after hearing what his men had done. Powerful, decisive. Almost giddy. Things were turning around.

When the messenger left and closed the door, Dumay started pacing again.

"Excellent," Dumay said. "We've sent them a message of strength. Now, we'll see what Mr. Martin does."

"He'll be coming," Wedge said.

"I would expect nothing less."

"What are you going to do?"

Dumay smiled at Wedge. "Me? Nothing. He'll never make it all the way here. You and the men will make sure of that."

"So, you do want me to deal with him."

"No, not the way you're implying. I already told you that, Mr. Wedge. Do not kill Heck Martin."

Wedge looked at him for a second. "Things have changed."

"Changed how? We beat up one cowboy."

Wedge smiled wryly. "Out here, Mr. Dumay, among folks such as these, a thing like that matters. Very much, in fact. You hurt one of theirs. Trust me. Everything has changed."

"Well, I like my odds."

"This Heck Martin, he's a fighter. He'll come at you now."

Dumay stopped pacing. He didn't like Wedge's use of the word *you*.

The killer continued, "And he'll keep coming until we kill him or he kills us."

Dumay leaned back at the suggestion. "Don't be ridiculous. We got rough with one man. In the mines, that's to be expected from time to time. As a mine owner, if you don't crack an employee's head every now and then—"

"This isn't a mine full of dirty-faced, broken men scratching at the walls like a bunch of tunnel rats, waiting for the roof to cave in on them. This is open country. And these folks are not your employees. Heck Martin is nobody's employee. Man like him, he'd sooner take a bullet than a yoke."

"What's your point?" Dumay snapped, feeling aggravated. "You sound like you admire the man."

"Admire him?" Wedge said thoughtfully. "No, but I respect him. And more to the point, I understand him. And like I said, you've changed everything. You're going to have to kill him now."

Dumay made a face. "Enough of your melodrama, Mr. Wedge. Ready the men. Tell them to intercept any trespassers, disarm them, and send them back to Hope City. Except Heck Martin. I want them to bring him to me."

"Where will I be?"

"Here, of course, protecting me. That's why I hired you, after all."

Wedge arched an eyebrow. "You think the men can stop Heck Martin and bring him to you?"

"Of course, I do. They're tough, and they're armed, aren't they? Besides, Martin understands I'm serious now. Mark my words. He'll be ready to listen to logic."

"You think so, huh? What if he doesn't want to come? And what if his men refuse to leave him behind?"

Dumay fluttered a hand with impatience. "Our men can beat them if they must, but I forbid them to shoot anyone. I will not have the reputation as a murderer."

Wedge chuckled humorlessly. "Your boys are brawlers, but Heck and his folks, they don't fight with fists. They fight with guns. Risky business, what you're asking."

"Risky? How? This is our territory. I own it legally and hold the title."

"Well, you be sure to hold up that piece of paper once the lead starts flying. I'm sure it will keep you safe."

"You came to me very highly recommended, Mr. Wedge, but if I didn't know better, I'd say you were afraid."

Wedge's face hardened. His pale eyes stared at Dumay.

Dumay squirmed, his blood chilling beneath the killer's gaze. "My apologies, Mr. Wedge. I—"

"A slight change in your wording, Mr. Dumay, and you would be dead now. Dead forever. I want you to understand that. Back in San Francisco, you tell a lot of people what to do. And like you said, sometimes, you have to crack some skulls. Out here, though? It's a different world. Maybe you're my boss. But let me be clear about something, Mr. Dumay. If you ever suggest that I'm a coward, I will put a bullet between your eyes. Do you understand?"

Dumay swallowed with difficulty. He was offended, angry even—no one talked to him that way—but those emotions withered away beneath the palpable menace of this rankled killer, who meant every word he'd said, Dumay realized.

"Yes, Mr. Wedge. I understand. And I apologize for—"

"Good. If you understand, we will be all right. Now, I'm going to go prepare the men for Heck Martin—as best I can, anyway." He turned toward the door.

"Excellent. And Mr. Wedge?"

Wedge half turned. "Yes?"

"Tell them to break Heck Martin's hands. I don't want him able to punch or pull a trigger. Break his hands and his fingers."

CHAPTER 20

As Heck thundered southward, he muzzled his emotions as best he could and forced his mind to think logically.

What he wanted to do, what his emotions told him to do, was to ride in there and shoot everybody.

But his mind understood that would be a good way to get killed or to kick off a full-blown war, which would get a lot of his people killed and likely cost him the valley and his life.

So as he drew nearer, he slowed Red and concealed the Colt in his lap.

Rounding the corner, he saw four men gathered together. They were burly types and stood there talking rather than sitting on their horses, which told Heck exactly what happened here.

These men weren't cowboys. They were Dumay's thugs, sent her to thump anyone who showed up.

Anger flared again in Heck, but this time, he controlled it more easily because he'd already done so on the ride and because the crucial moment was upon him, and if one thing set Heck apart from other men, it was his ability to perform under pressure.

To that point, as he rode closer, the world slowed for him even as his mind and body continued to operate at full speed.

The men looked up and saw him. A couple of them flinched. No one drew, but hands dropped to pistols or gripped rifle slings.

Fools.

Heck showed them a big smile and, gripping the reins in the hand that held the hidden Colt, raised his free hand in a friendly wave.

They didn't know what to do with that and basically just stood there, looking at him as he rode right up to them.

"Hi, fellas," Heck said, turning Red so they wouldn't see the pistol as he dismounted. "One of my men looks like he fell off his horse, and I was wondering if maybe you boys could give me a hand?"

He gave the statement a chipper lilt at the end, making it into a hopeful question as he came around the stallion, pistol low to his side, smiling like a moron.

A man with a scarred face and a swollen eye stepped forward, no doubt bolstered by Heck's friendliness, taking it for weakness, the way so many stupid men misinterpreted smiles. The man tightened his hands into fists.

Heck noticed the knuckles were swollen and bloody. "Where's Wyatt?"

"Wyatt?" Scarface chuckled. "Never heard of her."

Knowing he had to act quickly, Heck just smiled and

scanned the surrounding area but saw nothing. Maybe Wyatt had avoided the mix-up altogether.

"You Heck Martin?" Scarface demanded.

"Yeah, I'm Heck," Heck said, and dropped the man with a lightning-fast left hook to the jaw.

Scarface never saw it coming. It landed clean, spun his head around, and knocked him out. He dropped to the ground, one arm jutting stiffly up at a strange angle like the busted flagpole of a sacked fort.

"You draw, you die," Heck declared, putting his gun on the other men, who gasped with shock and regarded him with obvious fear. "I'm not playing with you savages. Get your hands in the air, or I'll kill you. That's it. All the way up."

The men complied, wide-eyed. Lifted high, their hands shook.

"You," Heck said, pointing to the closest one. "Reach down real slow and pull that shooting piece out of your belt."

"You ain't gonna shoot me, are you?"

"Not unless you do something stupid. That's it. Use just your thumb and forefinger. You try to get a grip on that thing, I will put a hole through your heart."

Handling the men one at a time, Heck disarmed all three, then had them step back from their guns and knives, which he gathered and loaded onto the men's horses. Then he led the horses over to Red and tied them to lead ropes.

The horses, sensing his authority and that of Red, were as docile as the men.

"Mister Martin," one of the men said, "those ain't even our horses. They belong to Mr. Dumay. If you take them—"

"Where's my calf?"

"Calf?" the man closest to Heck asked, doing a poor job of pretending ignorance. "What calf?"

Heck stomped on the man's knee. He felt it break—and heard it, too—and the man dropped to the ground, screaming, and clutching his busted leg with bloody hands.

They all had bloody hands. They'd all been in on it, had all beaten Dusty.

He walked over to the next man. "What happened to your hands? How did they get all bloody?"

"Oh—um—well..."

Heck slapped him across the face.

The man, clearly a fighter, surged forward with a sloppy punch.

Heck stepped away at an angle and clipped the man with a stiff jab that sent him reeling.

The final man panicked and ran forward toward his horse and weapons.

As the man reached the horse and stopped, Heck took careful aim and pulled the trigger. The .44 caliber ball punched through the man's boot, smashed his ankle, and dropped him to the ground, where he, too, screamed in pain.

Heck felt no remorse, considering what these men had done to Maguire.

"You boys got off easy," Heck told the man he'd only slapped and jabbed. "I've seen you now. I know who you are. Run for California while you still can. If my friend dies, I will kill all four of you. And tell Dumay the same thing. If my friend dies, I will kill him. Nothing will stop me. No defense, no protector, no amount of money will save him. That's a promise, and I always keep my promises. Do you understand?"

"Yes, sir," the man whimpered, all the fight having gone out of him.

On the southern horizon, a dozen riders were charging this way. They had heard the gunshot, no doubt.

"Head for the hills while you still have air in your lungs, boys," Heck said.

As Heck walked back to Red, the first man, the one with the scarred face and the bloodiest knuckles, sat up groggily and cursed at Heck.

As Heck passed, he kicked the man in the head, knocking him out again. Then he mounted up and rode north.

Behind him, still several hundred yards off, one of the approaching riders fired a shot from the back of his galloping horse, showing just how undisciplined they really were.

Which was good, of course, but also showed how this situation was boiling over.

What the men he'd just smashed had done, how he'd punished them, and how he handled this developing situation would either invite aggression from Dumay or discourage it.

That's the way it goes with any kind of fight. Turning points arise, demanding decisive action. React unwisely or too slowly or, worse yet, allow your opponent to get the tempo, and your chances fall apart.

But if you strike with speed, precision, and just the right amount of power, you can put your opponent—even a larger, more powerful man—on his heels, and set into motion a chain of events leading to his destruction.

How should he handle this situation?

He had hobbled a few men, taken their weapons and horses, and sent a clear message to them and Dumay.

But now, a bunch more were charging after him. And at least one of them was raring to pull a trigger.

Was Frank Wedge among them?

Whatever the case, Heck hoped to avoid further bloodshed.

But what if that was out of his hands? What if they demanded a gunfight?

Well, if that was the case, he was just going to have to kill all of them. And if he killed all of them, he would have to send his women and children into the fort, round up his fighting men, and launch an attack with the objective of surprising his enemies and killing both Dumay and Wedge.

With those two dead, these other men might lose the will to fight.

But Heck sure hoped it wouldn't come to that. He didn't want all that blood on his hands, and even though the brazen plan would be his best in that situation, he knew that many, perhaps even most of his people, would die in a fight like that. Dumay simply had too many men.

Then, as Heck rounded the corner, he nearly collided with a group of riders.

CHAPTER 21

"You all right, son?" Mr. Mullen, at the front of the pack, shouted.

Behind him, riding hard, were a few good men whom Heck trusted: Tom Mullen, Ray McLean, Titus Haines, and A.J. Plum.

"I'm all right," Heck said. "Got some fellas coming this way, though. And a few more hurting on the ground back there. Have you seen Wyatt?"

"Yeah, he came riding past on the far side of the canyon before we saw Maguire."

That was odd, but Heck didn't have time to give it any thought. He was just glad their friend was okay. "Did they take Maguire to Doc?"

"Yeah, Paul and Zeke took him." Mr. Mullen frowned. "He's hurt bad, Heck."

"I know. I pray to God Doc and Hope can save him. Otherwise, this whole valley will drown in blood."

The others arrived and wanted to know what happened.

"I'll tell you later. No time now. Everybody get up into the woods here, close to the edge, just around the bend. That's it. Get out of sight."

"Aw, shucks," A.J. Plum complained. "I wanted to fight."

"You might still get the chance," Heck said. He got them into the woods and explained what they were going to do.

He was surprised Dumay's men hadn't arrived yet. They probably stopped to check on the wounded thugs.

He hoped their condition struck fear into the hearts of the riders. The more hesitant they were, the easier they would be to break.

"How many riders are there?" Titus asked.

"A dozen, maybe more."

"We should all shoot as soon as they come around the corner," A.J. Plum said.

"Yeah," Abe agreed. "By they time they know what hit them, we'll reload and shoot them again. We could wipe them out before they even return fire."

Heck smiled. "You boys know how to fight, I'll give you that, but we can't just kill these men, not unless they force us to. Otherwise, we'll have that war we talked about. And we can't afford that."

"I agree, Heck," Mr. Mullen said. "We have too many women and children at the fort, not enough men. Dumay has three men to every one of ours."

"Which is a great reason to kill a dozen of them now," Plum said. "That'll even the odds a little."

Heck shook his head. "These men aren't fighters, most of them. They'll punch you in the face, but they've never fought with guns like we have. That's our biggest advantage. But if we kill a bunch of them, that might galvanize the survivors and set their fighting spirit on fire. Just follow my plan and be ready. Then, if they come around the corner and do start shooting, you just go ahead and do what you gotta do."

Heck reloaded his empty chamber and got into position beside a mound of boulders close to the bend.

A minute later, he heard the riders coming. They were moving fast but not full out.

Which meant they had stopped, and some of the wind had gone out of their sails.

How much wind, exactly?

They were about to find out.

The riders came around the bend.

Heck shot his Colt into air and drew the hammer back again. "Halt!"

His gunshot and voice both boomed with authority, and the riders slammed to a stop.

One man didn't stop in time. His horse collided with that of the man in front of him, smashing the lead rider's leg and pitching the second man from his saddle.

"No one move!" Heck shouted. "Look at the men behind me. Their rifles are ready to fire. Get your hands in the air."

As he spelled out the truth to the startled riders, he looked for familiar faces.

No sign of Dumay, no sign of Wedge.

These men were tense. Most looked terrified. A few looked jumpy. But they raised their hands.

Except one of them, who looked jumpier and surlier than the rest. He was a pug-nosed man with flashing eyes and a face full of freckles.

"Get your hands up," Heck told the man. "You draw, you die."

Freckles drew.

Heck shot him in the chest and drew back the hammer again in case a fight broke out.

It didn't.

Which told him a lot about these men, confirming his suspicions. They were thugs, not fighting men.

How different things might have been, had Wedge ridden with them. One man like that could change the behavior of those he rode with.

But Wedge was not here, and when Freckles tumbled to the ground, dead as a stone, none of the other men jumped.

Heck was pleased that none of his own men cut loose, either. That showed good discipline.

"I warned him," Heck said coolly. "I warned all of you."

Keeping their hands high in the air, the men nodded and muttered.

"You want us to shoot them, Heck?" A.J. Plum called out.

"Not unless they do something stupid," Heck replied, knowing the blacksmith had only asked to strike fear into Dumay's men.

"Look," one of the riders said. "We don't want no trouble. We was just doing what we was told."

"Listen up, all of you, because you need to hear this," Heck said. "Sometimes, just doing what you're told is a good way to get killed. This is one of those situations. You don't believe me, ask your buddy with the freckles."

A few of the men cast horrified glances at the dead man.

"He had no stake in this valley. None. Dumay just paid him.

Same goes for all of you. How long have you men even been riding for Dumay?"

"Just a couple of months," one man said. "Since we left San Francisco."

"So he paid you to come here and do this?"

Nods all around.

"Did he pay you enough to die?"

The heads quit nodding and started shaking.

"Because that's what's going to happen if you keep pushing us. Do you believe me?"

And just like that, they were back to nodding.

"Good. It's good you believe me. Believing me just might save some of your lives. You gotta figure out what's more important to you, working for Dumay or surviving. No matter what happens here, you men have no stake in this valley. We do. This is our home. And anybody who tries to take it is going to die. Do you understand?"

The men nodded again.

"Good. Now say it. Tell me what's going to happen if you keep pushing us? What are you going to do?"

"We are going to die," the men chorused.

It was Heck's turn to nod. "Truer words were never spoken. Now, we're gonna relieve you of your weapons and horses."

Dumay's men, having clearly taken Heck's words to heart, did not object.

Once he had confiscated their guns and horses, he sent them packing.

He wanted them to leave first, not his people. It sent a message.

And even more importantly, he wanted to see what they would do about the dead man.

Would they debate their options?

Carry him?

Drag him?

In the end, without a word passing between them, they abandoned the dead man and let him lie there like a clod of mud.

Which told Heck a lot about their character and the state of their union.

Some of these men were undoubtedly friends, but they were not a cohesive fighting force of men who viewed one another as brothers.

And that, Heck knew, was very good news.

CHAPTER 22

Dumay paced back and forth, his face burning with rage. He wanted to step outside and breathe some fresh air, but he didn't dare. After all, what if Heck Martin, who had clearly come unhinged, was waiting somewhere out there with a rifle?

Better to let this moment pass before taking chances like that.

But first he needed to understand the moment.

"So Heck Martin told you to stop, and you stopped, and he shot one of you, and the rest of you… did what, exactly?" With every word, he grew angrier. This wasn't supposed to happen. What was wrong with these men? "Other than letting him take your guns and horses… which were *my* horses, of course. Tell me. How did you let this happen?"

"It all happened so fast," one of the men mumbled.

"Yeah," another said. "He warned us not to touch our weapons, but Truby went for it."

"Next thing you know," a third man said, "Truby was dead. And I mean dead. By the time he hit the ground, he didn't even have any kick left in him."

The other men nodded.

"Never saw anything like it," one of them said. "Never saw anything half so fast. One second, we was riding. Next, Truby's down, and all we can say is 'yes, sir' and 'no, sir.' That Heck Martin's quick as a demon and twice as mean."

That got them all to nodding and stoked the fires of Dumay's rage. "Why didn't you do something?"

One of the men looked at Dumay like he was crazy. "Would you have?"

Dumay glared at the man. "I hired you to stand up to him."

"Yeah, but you didn't hire us to die."

Another man said, "Besides, we did stand up to him. But I'm not gonna lie. My guts turned to water out there. He warned us what would happen, then Truby tried him, and Truby died, just like that, just like Heck Martin said he would."

Another man nodded. "It was just weird. He said it, then it came true, like he spoke into existence. Like we were facing the wrath of God."

"Wrath of God?" Dumay snapped. "You men are a disgrace. I thought you were supposed to be tough."

One of the men who had backed down from Heck apparently wasn't so intimidated by Dumay. He stepped forward with his fists balled at his side. "You want to see how tough I am, Dumay?"

Dumay backpedaled, shocked and terrified.

"You take one more step, and you're a dead man," Frank

Wedge said from beside the door. His gun was on the angry man. "It's time for you to leave. All of you."

The men herded out the door.

The man who'd threatened Dumay paused in the doorway. "I'll leave, but I'm not coming back. I thought this was a good job, but I was wrong. This was just a good-paying job. Thing is, we stay here, we're all gonna end up dead."

"Nonsense!" Dumay shouted. He wanted to throttle the man. "We have a huge advantage in numbers."

"Just like we had today," one of the other men added. "Lot of good that did us. I'm with Hank. I'm heading out."

"Don't bother going back to San Francisco if you abandon me in my hour of need," Dumay snarled. "I'll see that you never get another job again!"

"With all due respect, sir," one of the men said, "if you don't leave this place, you won't live to see San Francisco again."

Despite his hot anger, Dumay felt a powerful chill, hearing these words. He did his best not to show it. "Is that what Martin said?"

"He said if anybody pushed, he would kill them."

"We'll see about that," Dumay said, "because I intend to push him off this land and out of this territory."

"Good luck, sir," a man who hadn't spoken until now said. "I'm with these men. I'm heading out. Look, Mr. Dumay, I appreciate the money you paid me, but you really ought to—"

"Shut up!" Dumay shouted. "Get out of my sight, you traitors!"

He didn't have to tell them twice. They marched off a short distance and started talking among themselves. A few seconds later, several other men joined them, listened, and glanced in his direction.

That was a problem. The last thing he needed was these men spreading fear and cowardice throughout the camp.

The same went for that first crew that had come in here, the ones who'd roughed up Heck Martin's friend.

Heck Martin had disarmed them, too, and battered them badly. The doctor was busy now doing what he could for the man who'd been shot through the foot and the one with the broken leg.

The two who could still walk had already left camp, taking a few others with them.

Wedge had urged Dumay to stop them, regardless of how he had to do it, but Dumay had pointed out the obvious: these weren't soldiers, they were merely employees. If they wanted to leave, they could leave.

Now, Wedge was at his side again. "You can't let these men leave, too."

Dumay glared at him. "I repeat, Mr. Wedge, these are employees, not soldiers. What would you have me do, shoot them?"

Wedge nodded calmly. "Yes, if need be. Though I wouldn't shoot them unless I had to. Better to lock them up for a while and talk to them. Then, if they didn't comply, yes, I'd kill them."

Dumay just stared at him. "You would do that? You would actually shoot these men?"

"Of course. You can see the effect they're having on the men. Look at the way those men keep looking at you. They're losing faith. Their love of gold is dying beneath their fear of Heck Martin."

"It will pass."

"Will it? I think you're one bad day away from a mass exodus. And then what will you do?"

"I..." Dumay's voice faded. What *would* he do if everyone abandoned him?

Seeing more of them glance in his direction, he closed the door.

Wedge had once again taken up his customary post, leaning against the wall beside the door. "Now are you ready for me to call out Heck Martin?"

"No."

"We kill him, his friends will lose their fighting spirit. Though it sounds like we'll have to kill the kid, too, the one they call Seeker."

"Do you hear yourself? Kill a kid?"

"Sir, with all due respect, that boy Seeker is more deadly than any of your miners."

Dumay snorted. "A thirteen-year-old boy?"

"Doesn't make any difference how old he is when he puts a bullet through your head. You hear Wyatt and these men. That boy is a killer. He's Heck Martin's adopted brother, and he grew up here, the son of a mountain man and an Indian woman. He's already killed several men, including the Indians who killed his parents. That makes him an enemy to take seriously."

"Well, I won't be murdering a child."

"You don't, that child might very well murder *you*."

Dumay scowled at him. "Again, Mr. Wedge, it strikes me that you have a superfluous flare for the dramatic."

"I have a flare for the truth. It only sounds dramatic because you don't want to hear it. And since I signed on to keep you alive, I must share the truth, even when it's inconvenient. At least let me kill Heck Martin."

"No. We must do this legally."

"He killed one of your men. What message are you sending to the rest if you don't retaliate?"

"They don't call the shots here, I do."

Wedge shrugged. "They might not call the shots, but they do make their own decisions. You heard those men. Some of them are quitting. If a few leave, don't you think others will follow? You must stop the flow before it sets to gushing, or you and I will be all alone here in the wilderness."

Dumay gritted his teeth. It was irritating, but Wedge was making sense. None of this was supposed to happen.

Of course, neither Wedge nor the others knew of Dumay's true plan or the brilliant next move he'd had in mind since he'd paved its way back in San Francisco.

Now, thanks to the cataclysmic events of today, he could finally initiate that move with maximum effectiveness. But it wouldn't do him any good if all his men deserted him before he could bring everything to fruition.

"What should I do, then?" he asked the killer. "Offer them more money to stay?"

Wedge shook his head. "This isn't about money. You're not asking these men to carry your suitcases. You're asking them to stand in the face of an enemy who is so far having his way with us. Let me kill him, and your troubles here will be over with very quickly."

"No. You may not kill him. I have to consider the aftermath, my reputation. Why are so determined to face him, anyway?"

Wedge's pale blue eyes twinkled. "Call it professional pride.

Heck Martin has never lost. I've never lost. We both cut a wide swath. Men like us, sooner or later, we have to see who's better."

"What a strange notion," Dumay said. "Whatever the case, my answer remains the same. You are not to call out Heck Martin unless I say so."

The twinkle went out of Wedge's eyes, but he didn't argue the point.

Dumay smiled and went to his desk and withdrew the envelope from beneath its blotter. "Besides, I have a better way."

He handed the envelope to Wedge, who read the name to which the letter inside was addressed. "Who's Randolph Harper?"

Dumay felt a surge of optimism just at the mention of the man's name. "Colonel Harper is an officer at Fort Laramie, two hundred miles to our east. Gather the best riders, give them the fastest horses, and send them to Fort Laramie to deliver this letter to the colonel. Provide extra horses so the riders can stay atop fresh mounts. There shouldn't be any trouble from Indians thanks to the Horse Creek Treaty. Riding hard, our men should reach Fort Laramie in five days. Also, make sure the men guarding the trail remain ready."

Wedge nodded. "I'll see to it. But didn't Wyatt say Heck Martin has a friend at Fort Laramie? An officer?"

Dumay dismissed Wedge's concern with a wave of his hand. "Colonel Harper isn't just an officer at Fort Laramie. He's the commanding officer. And wait until the colonel sees who wrote the letter I'm sending. The contents of that envelope cost me more than it cost to undermine Heck Martin's title and extract the mineral rights. Martin and his officer friend will be powerless against this letter."

CHAPTER 23

Heck and Hope sat to either side of Maguire's bed, each of them holding one of his rough hands.

Doc had given him medication for the pain, and Maguire had slipped once more into unconsciousness.

It was hard to look at the cowboy's face because it was so lacerated and distorted.

Heck had spent a good deal of time among bare-knuckle boxers, and he had never seen anyone so horribly disfigured.

According to Doc, however, Maguire's head wounds were less concerning than the damage to his torso.

Dumay's thugs had knocked Maguire down and kicked him brutally. His body was covered in their boot marks. They'd broken ribs but luckily hadn't punctured a lung. Still, there was bound to be internal damage and bleeding, and only time would tell how serious that might be.

Heck stared down at his friend with no expression, but inside, he raged like a grizzly.

He should have gut shot all four of those men and let them die slow, painful deaths.

That wasn't possible, of course, not unless he wanted to trigger an all-out war, but it's what they deserved for what they had done to Maguire.

The rest of Hope City seemed to agree. Maguire was very well liked, and everyone wanted vengeance for the unfathomably cruel beating he'd suffered. Even the badly frightened folks wanted to see justice.

Well, they would have it, Heck promised himself. They would have justice.

On Dumay, at least.

After all, it had been Dumay who'd given the command.

He had no doubt about that, no doubt that what happened to Maguire was a premeditated assault. Why else would those men have been waiting there instead of Dumay's cowpokes?

Yes, Dumay had arranged the beating.

And yes, Dumay would pay.

Heck didn't know how and didn't know when, exactly, but somehow, someday, he would pay.

"You will have justice, my friend," Heck said, giving Maguire's hand a light squeeze. "I promise you that. I promise that Dumay will pay for what he did to you."

Maguire stirred and groaned then slipped back into unconsciousness.

Hope released the patient's hand. "Come on, Heck," she whispered. "Let's let him rest."

Heck nodded, said another prayer for his friend, said goodbye to Doc, and left.

"It's hard to see him that way," Heck confessed outside.

"It is. He's always so full of life."

"Do you think he's going to make it, Hope?"

"I pray so. But I have no idea."

"What did Doc say?"

"He didn't, and I was afraid to ask. I know he's worried about internal bleeding, organ damage, and pneumonia."

"Does Doc have everything he needs? Should we send for anything?"

Hope shook her head. "I think he's all set. We can ask him later to make sure. Whatever the case, Maguire is in God's hands now."

Heck nodded. "I know. And I'll keep praying for him. But it's hard waiting, not knowing."

"Yes, it is."

They reached their cabin. Before going inside, Heck glanced around the compound.

Folks stood atop each tower, scanning the surrounding area.

To the south, Heck's drovers had brought in the herd despite the mostly depleted grass closer to home. Given the day's events, he wouldn't chance leaving anyone near Dumay's line.

The gate remained open. That way, if someone sounded the alarm, folks could move in and out and get into position before Dumay's forces arrived.

Despite his boiling anger and the horrible injuries his friend had sustained, Heck felt optimistic about their chances—more optimistic, certainly, than he'd had reason to feel when he'd awakened this morning.

Dumay had pushed.

Heck had pushed back... hard.

He had controlled his use of force, but he neither hesitated nor overreacted when the situation had warranted the use of deadly force.

He'd taken men out of the fight, confiscated many weapons and sixteen horses, and sent a clear message not just to Dumay but also to his employees.

Heck and his friends would fight.

Holding the door for Hope, he asked, "Where's Tor?"

"Mother has him."

"House always seems so empty without him."

Hope nodded. "It does. But we're not alone." She smiled and rubbed her swollen belly.

Heck crouched down and kissed her tummy and spoke to the baby growing inside. "I love you, baby. I love you so very much, and I promise to protect you no matter what."

Hope ran a hand through his hair. "What are you going to do, Heck?"

He stood and went to the coffee pot and sloshed it around and raised one eyebrow to his wife.

"No, thanks. You go ahead."

Heck nodded at her and poured the last of the coffee into his mug, saying, "It's time to push. Not necessarily today, but soon. We have to hit them again before they recover from today."

"Won't that just stir them up?"

"It's a good question," he said, "and you're right. We don't want to hit them too hard. We don't want them all coming at us at once. They're just scared enough to try to massacre us."

Hope shuddered. "Is that possible?"

"Sure, it's possible, but I don't expect it. And if they try, a whole bunch of them are going to die. Point is, we don't want them coming at us like that. We hurt them today. Hurt their morale. And we disarmed a bunch of them and took their horses, too. If we push them right now, some will tuck their tails and bolt."

"You mean leave the valley?"

He nodded. "They're thugs, not soldiers. Thugs are fine for an overwhelming attack, which is what we need to avoid triggering, but how will they hold up over the long haul?"

"It'll be getting colder soon," Hope said. "And the game will disappear. Maybe just wait for them to get cold and hungry?"

Heck smiled. "My wife, the strategist. You're right. Discomfort will wear on them. But we have to stay busy, have to keep at them, have to help them understand that they're in over their heads. The longer this conflict stretches out, the more they'll see that. Let them get cold and hungry. Let them get tired. Let them miss the city and friends and women and the rest of it. And every man who breaks will weaken the others."

"But if that starts to happen, won't Dumay just send them at us all at once?"

"He might. But I doubt it. Dumay talks tough, but he's the richest man in California. Could be he's here for the gold, but I think he's mainly here because I slighted him, selling the nugget to *Don* Vasquez."

Hope laughed, shaking her head. "Why didn't you sell it to him, anyway?"

Heck shrugged his shoulders. "Guess I didn't like his attitude."

"Mr. Martin, sometimes, I don't know about you."

"Yes, you do. You always know about me."

"That's true. But you have your ways."

"I do. Would you change that?"

"No, sir, I would not. Not one iota."

"I feel the same way about you, ma'am. But let me get going here."

"Not yet, Mister. You sit down and let me make something to go with that coffee."

"All right," he said, and took a seat at the table. "I guess it won't hurt to put something in my stomach. But then, I'm gonna take care of business. It's time to start fighting like Indians."

"What do you mean?"

"Well, we can't just ride in there, guns blazing. We have to fight smart. You don't see Indians just charging a bunch of cavalry troopers. They hit and run, inflicting damage and avoiding casualties as best they can. They whittle away, working on the enemy's nerves."

Hope studied him, her beautiful green eyes sparkling with intelligence and determination. "And that's what you want to do to Dumay? Hit and run?"

Heck nodded and knocked back the last of his coffee. "Among other things. There are more weapons than just bullets and knives and fists. We gotta take aim at their hearts and minds. We need to demoralize them, make them afraid to fight, make them want to quit. Let fear spread among their ranks."

"How do you expect to do that? What are you planning to do to them?"

Heck smiled at his wife. "Well, first…"

CHAPTER 24

"Should it be this cold?" William Brett complained, trudging through the wet grass of the valleys north of the camp. "It's only August, right?"

"September," Ethan said.

"Still. Must be in the forties," William said with a shudder.

"All this walking, we'll warm up," Garrett grumbled. "My back still hurts from the trail."

"Sleeping on the ground doesn't help. I never thought I'd say it, but I miss the flophouse back in Frisco. Fleas and all."

"Quit your bellyaching," Sapp told them. "We got a job to do."

"So says the only man on a horse," William said. He'd noticed that ever since Mr. Wedge had named Sapp the leader of their quartet, Sapp had completely changed.

Two days ago, Sapp would've been complaining louder than anyone. Now, he was acting like a foreman back in the mine.

Give some men a little power, it went straight to their heads.

And what right did Sapp have to lead them? Did they elect him? No. Was he smarter? No. Braver? Again, no. Sapp was completely unremarkable save for the fact that Wedge had picked him at random.

Everybody understood that. Everybody except Sapp, that was.

He was acting like God's anointed.

"We'll get the horses back," Sapp said, trying a chipper, condescending tone that annoyed William. "The horses and everything else. You'll see."

"Will I?" William said.

"Yes," Sapp said.

"How do you know, Sapp?" William said. "How do you know I'll even be here one more day? What if I hike out of here like the others?"

Sapp's mouth fell open, making him look even stupider than he was. "You would desert Mr. Dumay?"

"Desert? This isn't the army, Sapp," Ethan chimed in.

"That's right," Garrett said. "I didn't sign no contract. I'm my own man."

"Me, too," William said, feeling the thrill of rising against their poorly chosen leader.

Truth be told, he hadn't really been thinking of leaving, but it was exciting to consider and fun to watch Sapp struggle.

When life hands you lemons, it's fun to squirt the juice in somebody's eye.

"I agreed to come here, chase off some squatters, and help Dumay get his mine started," William said, letting Sapp have it. "Not freeze and stand watch in the dark like a soldier. The squatters are still here. And where's Dumay's mine?"

"Yeah," Ethan said. "And now people are getting killed."

"Not people," Sapp said. "Just one person, Ericson."

"Serves him right," Garrett said. "Ericson always did think he was special."

"Well, he ain't special now," Sapp laughed, temporarily forgetting his duty to tow the company line. "He's just dead."

"I was talking to Mort," William said. "He was there that day. Said Ericson never stood a chance. Said Heck Martin shot him before he could even clear his pistol."

Garrett nodded. "Killed him dead. One shot."

"And he really thumped those other boys," Ethan said. "Even Hodges. And Hodges is nobody I'd want to mess with."

"Nope, not the others, either," Garrett said. "Back in Frisco, I saw Chalfont whip two men at the same time."

"But Heck Martin busted up all four of them at the same time," William said. "Four of them, just like there's four of us."

Nobody said anything for a moment, and William knew his comment had hit home.

How couldn't it? Here they were, four average fellows, trudging toward the exact spot where four much tougher men had gotten thrashed by Heck Martin alone—and not far from where another man had gotten gunned down.

What if Heck Martin was waiting for them at the boundary between the valleys? What if he had a bunch of killers with him? What if he had that crazy half-breed kid with him, the one Landers said scalped a dozen people.

"I don't like it here," Ethan confessed. "Feels like we're all gonna die here."

"That's enough of that sort of talk," Sapp said, but in the

predawn gloom, his face looked pale and frightened, almost ghostly.

"Porter and them left in the night," Garrett said.

"What?" Sapp said, sounding shocked. "Milo Porter?"

Garrett nodded. "Yup. But you didn't hear it from me. Porter and those other two who always hang around with him."

"His cousins."

"I don't know if they're kin or what. I just know they left."

"Pshaw," Sapp said. "They didn't leave."

"Did so," Garrett said, sounding angry. "I seen them in the night, packing out. And that one boy with the curly hair, he looked like he was carrying half the camp out on his back."

"Mr. Dumay will be angry about that," Sapp said. "Deserting is one thing. Stealing supplies, though? That's downright criminal."

William laughed. "What's Dumay gonna do? Call for the police?"

"He might send Mr. Wedge after them," Sapp said.

"Shoot," William said. "He won't send Wedge. Haven't you noticed? Since we got here, Dumay keeps Wedge real close."

"Probably afraid Heck Martin will get him otherwise," Ethan said.

"I'd be afraid, too," William said. "I hear Heck Martin said he's gonna kill Dumay."

"If his friend dies," Sapp corrected him. "The one they beat up."

"That was a dumb move," Garrett said. "If we're gonna run them off, we should run off. Not sit around poking them."

"Mr. Dumay has his reputation to consider," Sapp said. "He's a famous man. Very wealthy and respected. He can't just go and attack these people. Women, children. How would that look?"

"It would look better than us getting killed out here," Garrett said.

"Dumay cares more about his reputation than he does our lives," William said. He'd started this whole gripe mostly as a diversion, but the more he talked, the more he believed what he was saying.

"It's no wonder folks are leaving," Ethan said and cast a longing glance into the western darkness. "I miss home."

"That's enough of that kind of talk," Sapp said, apparently remembering his laughable duty again. "Those deserters are fools. They'll never make it home alive."

"Porter will," Garrett said. "Porter's tough as nails."

"If Porter was tough, he would still be here," Sapp declared.

"Wrong, Sapp," William countered. "Sticking around here wouldn't make Porter tough. It would make him stupid."

"Yeah, stupid and maybe dead," Garrett said.

Rain had fallen in the night. Not much. But enough that the grass was wet.

William's worn-out boots had soaked through. Now his feet were cold and wet. Nothing makes a man more miserable than cold, wet feet.

They walked in discontented silence, each man lost to his own swirling thoughts, until they passed Dumay's small herd of cattle and came to the weak campfire of the night guard, who headed south in a hurry.

Only one of them lingered, a tall, bucktoothed guy William had seen around. The guy's eyes were wide. They rolled across the dark bulk of the wooded slope to the west.

"Spooky night, boys," he said. "Keep your rifles ready. Something's moving out there. And by something, I mean a bunch of somethings. Sounds like people, you want to know the truth."

With that, he hurried after the others.

"Oh, man," Ethan said. "What if it's Heck Martin and that crazy kid?"

"I got no fight with them," Garrett said. "They didn't do nothing to me."

William realized he was nodding. "This is a bad situation."

"Those boys got spooked by squirrels, I bet," Sapp said, but with dawn breaking to the east, the man's face looked more frightened than ever. Then, suddenly, as the light broke over the mountains and shone across the field, illuminating the opposite slope, Sapp's face went from frightened to terrified.

William followed his gaze to the edge of the forested slope, where a wooden sign stood. The red paint of its message had dripped, making it look like blood.

Suddenly, William's feet weren't the only thing that was cold. His heart had iced over.

"What's it say?" Sapp asked.

The others looked to William, knowing he'd had some schooling.

"It says, 'Stay and starve, or leave and live.'"

CHAPTER 25

After a solid hour of spying on Dumay's camp, Heck and Abe Zale, the former woodcutter and present-day cattleman, started back across the ridge toward home.

"Seems like there's less of them than there were," Abe said.

"I had the same thought," Heck said. "Maybe some of them are coming to their senses and heading back to California."

For the last few days, they had been patiently whittling away at the miners' nerves with signs, letters floated downstream, and by stomping around in the woods when Dumay's men were standing guard on the border.

Heck had also mustered a large group and rode into view of a four-man watch and paused there, letting reality settle onto the men like a wagonload of grave dirt.

Dumay might have superiority in numbers, but those four men were completely at the mercy of Heck and his three dozen riders, who sat there, staring across the waving grasses at the terrified quartet.

A number of Heck's men, outraged by the attack on Maguire, wanted to quit poking and start shooting.

But Heck refused. They had to stay patient and couldn't let anger or pressure or anything else trick them into doing something rash.

That's how you get hurt.

It was a lesson he'd learned in the ring. Then frontier life had burned the same lesson into him, making it a part of him.

Never let tension cloud logic. No matter how bad things get, you have to stand steady and do whatever makes the most sense in that moment.

That's the key to success and survival alike.

You have to stare reality square in the face, then react to what's real, not what you wish was real.

Which was hard sometimes.

Like now, when Heck's friend was lying in bed, fighting for his life.

Getting closer to home, they were passing through the big timber, where they'd been grazing cattle since backing off the lower valleys. The longhorns had devoured the grass and torn up the loam.

"Looks like a herd of pigs were rooting here," Abe said.

"The grass up here's different," Heck said. "It's the soft ground. Cows pull up the grass instead of cropping it."

"They really tore it up," Abe said. "We get a heavy rain, we're gonna lose a lot of topsoil."

Heck nodded, remembering how heavy rain and flooding had devastated mountain farms back home in Kentucky.

"I thought maybe the herd could graze here for a while and give our grass time to grow back. But they're tearing it all up, and there just isn't enough grass up here, not for a herd this size. We need those valleys to the south."

"Dumay probably knew that all along," Abe said. "He's hoping we'll try to push onto his ground. That would give him the legal right to defend his property."

Heck thought for a second. "You're probably right. I'll bet that's just what he's been hoping for, the whole reason he bought that ground in the first place. It's like he knew everything about us even before he got here, almost like he had somebody set up here, studying us, reporting back to him."

"Who would do something like that?"

"A spy."

"A spy? Like who?"

"I have no idea."

"Well, he's got the snakes, Pulcher and Boon."

"Could be it was them."

"But you don't think so?"

"No," Heck admitted, "I guess I don't. Jem and Trace could have told him some things, but they left a long time ago. They could have told him about the location of the cave, but Dumay also knew about the road and the valleys and the cattle."

"So you think we have a spy in town?"

"Could be. Whatever the case, Dumay is playing this thing carefully. I think that's just what he's hoping to do: starve our cattle, hoping it'll trigger a clash on the border. Then he could send everybody in here, guns a blazing. It's their only chance. One big attack."

"So what are you going to do, Heck?"

Heck didn't say anything for a moment. He knew what he

had to do. He just didn't want to do it. "I want you to round up some of the older steers."

"All right. How many?"

"Ideally, in country like this, we should have at least four acres of good pasture per cow. So, a herd this size, we could use about five thousand acres."

"How many do we have?"

"We're about a thousand acres short. Divide that by four, and you realize we need to unload around two hundred and fifty of our oldest steers."

Abe lifted his eyebrows. "You sure that's smart, Heck? We still got a lot of young stuff. You'd make more money if we held them another year or two."

"I'm sure. This way, the rest of the herd will have enough to eat. That'll take away Dumay's power against our herd."

"All right. I'll get the boys on it."

"I'll tell Burt. He'll drive them."

"I'll ride with him."

"Good. Bring however many men you think you need."

"Hate to leave you if Dumay comes a charging."

"He does, we'll handle it. You boys go ahead. Major Scotts-dale will appreciate the beef."

"Any messages for the man?"

"Yeah, we need to tell him what's happening. I'll write up a letter. Then we'll see what he says. Avery's a good man and might have some insight."

CHAPTER 26

Major Avery Scottsdale was just leaving the mess hall when Corporal Ennis stopped in front of him and saluted.

"Sir, I thought you'd like to know that some riders just came in an hour ago. They're talking about a friend of yours, sir."

"What friend?" Avery asked the young man.

"Heck Martin, sir."

"Is that right?" Avery felt like smiling at the mention of the enigmatic young mountain man, but he also understood that in country such as this, far-reaching talk usually meant bad news. "Are they having Indian trouble?"

"I don't think so, sir. These men, they didn't seem to be friends of Heck's."

"Bring them to me."

"They're gone, sir."

"Gone? They just got here."

"Yes, sir. They got here, went to see Colonel Harper, and then rode back out again."

Avery rubbed his jaw. It was late enough in the afternoon that his fingers met sandpaper. "Pretty late in the day to just turn around. Must have been in quite a hurry."

"Yes, sir."

"I wonder what they wanted with Colonel Harper?"

He didn't have to wait for an answer. Before Corporal Ennis could shed light on Avery's confusion, the commander summoned him.

Avery reported to Harper's office. "You wanted to see me, sir?"

"Yes, Major Scottsdale. Come in, come in. Sit down."

"Thank you, sir," Avery said, taking a seat across from his gray-haired commander.

"I just received two letters, Major. One was from a man named Percival Dumay. Have you heard of him?"

"No, sir."

"Well, as I understand it, he's the wealthiest man in California. Which apparently has given him certain influence, considering the source of the second letter. General Bradbury himself is asking us to intervene in a situation. It's not an official order, but…"

Colonel Harper spread his hands.

Avery nodded. "But it might as well be official, considering it's coming from General Bradbury."

"That's correct." Harper stared down at the envelope and shook his head. "Apparently, this Dumay recently moved into the territory. He's two hundred miles to the west, and he's having trouble with a friend of yours."

"Heck Martin, sir?"

"That's right. The general wants the cavalry to drive Martin from the land... by force if necessary."

Avery was confused. "Drive him out? Sir, Heck owns that land. And I don't mean he just staked a claim. He went through the proper channels and holds the title. He and Jim Bridger told me all about it last September, when they were here, helping us with the Horse Creek Treaty."

Harper frowned. "I keep thinking about what a great help those men were to us. Those Indians were getting restless until Martin and Bridger showed up. And there sure were a lot of them. Ten thousand. Things could've gone either way."

"I believe they could have, sir. Would have, even, if it weren't for Heck and Bridger. Their knowledge of the Indian languages and cultures and their reputation among the tribes is second to none. They saved Fort Laramie—not to mention a major war between the U.S. Army and the plains Indians."

"And now we must repay the favor by driving Heck Martin out of his valley."

"Are you certain there isn't some mistake, sir? Heck's never been anything but the best of the best in my experience, and again, it's my understanding that he holds the title to twenty-four square miles out there."

Harper sighed. "I don't like it any better than you do, Major, but there's nothing I can do about it. General Bradbury has spoken. And you know General Bradbury."

"Yes, sir."

General Nathaniel Bradbury was seldom seen on the frontier, but his influence remained powerful indeed. His battlefield was in Washington D.C., where he spent his days surrounded by cronies, rooting ever more deeply into the world of politicians and lobbyists, enjoying the high life at their expense.

For Bradbury to take a personal interest in some small affair in the wilderness was remarkably strange and could mean only one thing.

A politician had asked him to intervene.

And this wealthy Californian, Dumay, had likely lined that politician's pockets with money.

But why?

If you were the wealthiest man in California, why would you risk your life in this rugged country? Why tangle with the likes of Heck Martin? And why get politicians involved?

Dumay must have arranged everything prior to leaving California. So this was a premeditated move on his part.

Why?

Then Avery had it.

Heck's gold.

Heck had sworn Avery to secrecy then told him about the massive nugget he'd found and taken to San Francisco—and much of what had ensued there in that corrupt town.

By some means, Dumay had learned of the gold and followed Heck back, meaning to dig a mine.

But of course, he could share none of this with Colonel Harper without betraying Heck's trust, a thing he would not do.

"This Dumay is a clever one," Harper said with a thoughtful expression. He picked up the envelope and rapped its edge crisply against his desk. "He claims to own the mineral rights beneath Martin's land."

"Even if he does, sir, Heck doesn't have to give him access, correct?"

"Absolutely correct. Which is why I say Dumay is clever. He must have done his research concerning this region—and us."

"Us, sir?"

"That's right. What is the most difficult part about your job, Major? What makes supplying this fort so difficult?"

That was easy. "Our remoteness, sir."

"Exactly. And what provision do you have the hardest time securing? By which, I mean what provision costs us the greatest number of man hours?"

Again, the answer was instantaneous. "Firewood, sir."

"Yes, as this Percival Dumay must have learned. Because General Bradbury has approved a firewood contract with Dumay, along with a special right-of-way granting him unlimited access to Heck Martin's property."

"He's going to cut Heck's timber?"

"I won't guess at what he'll actually do, but yes, that's how our clever Mr. Dumay managed to gain unlimited access to Heck's Valley—and whatever lies beneath the surface. He no doubt expects to find gold or silver or some other precious commodity."

"Undoubtedly, sir. But does he have the right to mine? If this is a timber contract..."

Harper nodded, still frowning. "Dumay's lawyers must be awfully clever, as well. I've gone over the contract three times. It imposes no limits on Mr. Dumay. Ostensibly, it is a firewood contract, but as I read it, the contract grants him unrestricted access and use. He could legally dig a mine right through the floor of Heck Martin's kitchen."

Good luck with that, Avery thought. *Those lawyers might be clever, but they clearly have never met Heck Martin.*

"May I read the contract, sir?"

"Certainly," Harper said, handing him the envelope. "I don't like this anymore than you do, Major, but we are soldiers and must do our duty, whether we like it or not."

"Yes, sir."

"Read that at your leisure, Major. And in the meantime, get to work preparing supplies for an expedition to Heck's Valley."

CHAPTER 27

"You can count on me, Heck," Burt said. "Bickle Freighting finds a way."

"I know I can, Burt. You're a good man."

Heck patted Burt on the shoulder. He hadn't meant it to be a hard blow, Burt knew, but it jarred him heavily.

He couldn't imagine getting punched by Heck. No thank you. The man towered over everyone with shoulders as wide as an ox's yoke.

But Heck didn't just have size. He was the most powerful man Burt had ever met. You could feel strength coming off him the way you could with a top-notch draft animal, but there was no wagon-puller in Heck. Sure, he had strength and grit, but he wasn't just tough. He was smart, too, a thinker, more of a predator than an ox.

On top of all this, he was a natural leader who cared about his people, and God had never created a better friend. Burt sure was grateful to Heck, who had saved the party from certain death then given Burt a chance to start a business here, a business that was now thriving.

Which all made Heck a man you couldn't help but want to please.

Burt himself had always been headstrong and independent, a man determined to make his own way in the world and build up a business and a name that would echo across the West and down through time.

Even Burt, however, found himself wanting to please this smiling and sometimes savage giant.

Well, there was nothing so wrong with that, was there? Burt would always be his own man, but he understood that Heck was the rightful leader of this valley, not him, and he was the one man whose orders Burt had never minded following.

"I'll get them to Laramie, get the best price I can, deliver your message, and come home carting whatever this Avery Scottsdale tells me."

"Thank you, Burt. You're the only person I'd trust with this job."

They shook hands, and Burt was surprised, as always, by the size and strength of Heck's hand. It was like shaking hands with a grizzly.

The citizens of Hope City cheered Burt as he and the others rode off atop horses, heading north with 250 steers. Two miles on, they would hit the trail, take a right, and drive the cattle east toward Fort Laramie.

Which was a familiar trip to Burt now, though he usually drove wagons instead of cattle.

Four men—Abe Zale, Zack Prentiss, Bill Derry, and Shorty

Potter—rode with him. They were in high spirits, calling back and forth as they pushed the cattle up the road.

A pair of steers promptly broke away from the herd and took the lead.

Burt smiled.

Those two steers had just made his job much easier. He'd bet his bottom dollar that they would lead the others all the way to Laramie.

Burt always loved being on the trail. It was who he was. And that excitement filled him now.

He never worried about the inevitable obstacles that would crop up along the way. *Bickle Freighting finds a way* wasn't just a business slogan, after all, it was his mindset.

He wished they had wagons, too. It would be good to sell items to straggling emigrants along the way and unload the rest at Fort Laramie and even better to stock up on whatever Fort Laramie had to offer and bring it back to his friends and neighbors.

But that wasn't possible this time. Heck couldn't spare any additional men, so Burt and the other four drovers all had to mind the herd.

So they'd packed light, filling bags and panniers that bounced behind their saddles as they trotted ever northward.

Approaching the junction with the trail, Burt scanned the way ahead, watching for trouble. A freighter always looked ahead, always read the signs if he wanted to keep his hair in this country, but with Dumay's men in the land, caution was more important than ever.

Seeing no sign of the miners, Burt drove the lead steers onto the rutted trail and turned right toward Fort Laramie.

Behind him trotted the two-hundred and fifty steers. Trailing and flanking them, the four drovers kept the steers moving and rounded up those who started to drift.

If this early going was an indication of how the herd would behave over the next two hundred miles, Burt figured he was in for the smoothest trip of his life.

Then they entered the gap between two low hills, and a volley of gunfire erupted above them.

A bullet tugged at his sleeve. Burt hunched low and spurred his horse.

One of the lead steers was down, blatting horrible, and the other had broken off at a hard angle, seeking the scrub.

Behind them, the cattle lowed and shuffled and broke, stampeding after the lead steer, who crashed into the trailside brush as another volley cracked from above.

Burt saw the bloom of smoke among the rocks and saw men here and there popping up to fire before quickly disappearing behind cover again.

He saw their blocky bodies and mustaches and red shirts and knew they were Dumay's men.

There was no sense in returning fire, but when he turned, Abe Zale was doing just that, firing up at the attackers. Abe's sleeve was torn and bloody.

Behind him, chaos ruled.

The second volley had killed or wounded several steers and turned the herd again, breaking it into a few fragments that rushed off in various directions.

As Burt comprehended this disaster, he saw a wall of panicked steers crash into Bill Derry, whose horse wheeled, rearing.

Derry fell hard to the ground and disappeared for a time within the dusty cloud and blurry forms of the stampeding cattle.

More gunshots cracked behind Burt as he rushed forward to help the fallen man.

Zack Prentiss beat him there, and Burt felt a glimmer of hope, seeing Prentiss help Derry off the ground and onto his horse.

Derry's own steed had galloped off the trail and away from the sprinting steers.

Burt hollered to Abe and rode after the herd.

A bullet whizzed by, close enough to hear, and Burt stayed low and rode out of the gulley, around the bend, and out of sight of the snipers.

He rode over to Prentiss and Derry.

Prentiss raved, cursing Dumay's snipers, wild with fear and anger.

Derry smiled crazily, no doubt shocked to be alive after falling into a stampede. He hunched atop Prentiss's horse, obviously hurting. He had a big scrape on one cheek, his left arm hung lifelessly at his side, likely the result of a dislocated shoulder, and his other arm clutched his side, where he probably had some broken ribs. But it was nothing short of miraculous that he had survived at all.

Abe and Shorty Potter joined them then, bringing further relief.

A bullet had grazed Abe, who ranted in a fighting frenzy, wanting to unleash his fury on Dumay's thugs.

Shorty, like Burt, had escaped uninjured. The cowboy

leaned and spat, looking remarkably calm. "Well, that didn't go so good."

Burt didn't know the man well but quickly took measure of him, recognizing his rock-solid character. "Shorty, get everybody home."

Shorty nodded. "All right, boss."

"Home?" Abe shouted. "We can't let them get away with this. We gotta circle around behind them and let them have it."

Burt shook his head. "There are too many of them, and they have all the advantages. Live to fight another day, Abe. Go back and tell Heck. We'll get them."

"What about the steers, boss?" Shorty asked.

"Shorty, Abe, let's cut the steers off and see how many we can round up," Burt said. "We won't get them all, but we'll save those we can. The others will probably run straight to Dumay's upper camp. It's only a quarter mile west of here. Derry, can you stand the pain if you and Prentiss stay a while? We need someone to keep watch."

Derry nodded grimly. "You do what you gotta do, boss. We'll keep an eye out."

Burt and the others went after the steers. Half an hour later, they'd rounded up most of the cattle.

Without doing a precise head count, Burt reckoned they'd recaptured a hundred and eighty or a hundred and ninety head.

Which was better than losing the herd but still made him burn with indignation.

Dumay's snipers had killed several steers, wounded another dozen—some so severely that they would need to be put down —and chased off a thousand dollars' worth of cattle.

It was a heinous act and a tremendous blow to Burt, who prided himself on always completing his mission.

Well, he wasn't through yet.

It wasn't possible to get the cattle through, obviously, but Heck wanted him to take more than steers to Fort Laramie.

"They were waiting on us," Burt said. "I don't know how, but they must have known we were coming."

Shorty leaned and spat again. "Either Dumay is a genius, or we have a spy in our midst."

The men all nodded. In the silence that followed, Burt stewed in his bitterness, knowing he had to announce his failure.

"I sure would like to deliver these steers," Burt said, "but if we try to drive the cattle north of the trail, the terrain will cause us trouble, and I'm sure Dumay's men will come after us. The whole reason they're here is to keep us from reaching Fort Laramie."

"Good," Abe said. "Let the cowards come. Let them try to fight us out in the open."

Burt shook his head. "There are too many of them. And if they stampede the cattle again, we'll lose more steers. We gotta cut our losses and head home."

"Prentiss," Burt said, when Shorty was ready to drive the steers back to Hope City, "you and Derry keep riding double, all right?"

"Sure thing, Burt."

Burt caught up the reins of Derry's horse. "I'm gonna borrow your horse for a spell if it's all right by you, Derry."

"No problem, Burt. I don't plan on riding anytime soon. Now that the excitement's worn off, I don't feel so hot." He smiled through the pain. "Feel like I got stomped by a stampede."

"Have Doc take a look at you," Burt said, edging away.

"Where are you going?" Abe said.

"Fort Laramie. I told Heck I'd deliver his letter to Major Scottsdale, and by gum, I'm gonna do it."

"I'll come with you," Abe said.

"Not a chance. No offense, my friend, but you'd slow me down. This is a one-man job."

"What about Dumay's men?"

"I'll head north a way before turning west then ride real fast."

"What if they come after you?"

Burt grinned at him. "Bickle Freighting finds a way!"

CHAPTER 28

William Brett was sweating like a pig. His heart
pounded furiously, his whole body trembled, and his
mouth tasted like he'd been chewing an iron bar.

He spat, but his mouth was too dry to expel anything but a
small, pink wad.

He licked his lips, touched them, and stared at the feather of
bright red blood smeared across his finger.

That's when he became aware of the throbbing pain, which
he soon realized he'd bitten in his panic.

How horrified he had been.

It had been terrible enough, squatting there in the rocks
with his rifle, charged with repelling Heck Martin's herd.

His mind had reeled with nightmare possibilities.

Then, when Clarkson had called out, "Here they come!" and
William had peered over the rocks and seen the approaching
dust cloud, his guts had turned to water.

Nearby, someone had laughed nastily, but for William,

everything was terror.

Then they had shown up, and William had angled his barrel vaguely in the direction of the herd and pulled the trigger. The musket had kicked him in the shoulder and clouded his vision with black powder smoke as rifles boomed beside him, and men shouted, and his mind whirled with fear.

When the smoke had cleared, he saw the cattle slamming this way and that and saw riders through the dust. One fell from his horse and disappeared beneath stampeding cattle. Another shouted with rage and fired up at the rocks.

William had flattened himself behind the boulder, frightened out of his wits.

Was Heck Martin down there? Was he coming for them now?

Behind him, he heard men yelling his name and knew they wanted him to reload and continue the fight, but he was too frightened. If they wanted to kill and die, let them. He was done.

After the shooting was over, he grunted when a boot slammed into his ribs.

He cursed and rolled over and saw Jem Pulcher glaring down at him.

"Get up, coward," Pulcher said. "They're gone."

William got up and joined the other men, who stood around in a strange group. Some looked angry. Some were laughing and clapping each other on the back. Several looked frightened. Others looked stunned. One man trotted off and heaved behind a boulder.

The laughers dominated the center of the group, recounting the skirmish with glee.

"I killed two cows," one man boasted.

"You see that one boy fall off his horse?" another laughed.

"Yeah," Pulcher said, "I thought he was a goner, but he got lucky. Wish they'd stomped him to death."

William blinked at the men and understood that the gulf between them and him was wider than the distance between the East Coast and the West.

He was no altar boy. He knew that. He'd lived a rough enough life, stealing and scamming and yes, fighting. He'd never backed down from a fight, not even when the odds were long.

But that had been fist fighting.

This was something altogether different. Something that was not part of him.

And these men, Pulcher and his cackling buddies, they hadn't just borne up under the moment; they had loved it. Shooting at people and cows had brought them to life in some way that William had never witnessed, some way he knew he, personally, would never experience.

And with this realization came another. He was done here. Done with these people. Done with this work. He wouldn't stay another day, not for all the gold in the world.

Because for as much as these men had enjoyed shooting, they hadn't performed all that well. Sure, they'd killed a few cows and stampeded the rest, and Post swore he'd wounded the one who turned and started returning fire, but none of the enemy were killed, not even the one who'd fallen beneath the stampede.

What did that mean?

Everything had changed again.

Heck Martin would come for them. And he and his men had done a lot more of this sort of fighting than these chuckling idiots.

Lately, William had heard several stories about Heck and his people, how they'd killed bandits and traitors and a whole bunch of Indians, and how Heck Martin had killed a giant grizzly with a Bowie knife.

Could Jem Pulcher or any of these men do those things?

Not a chance.

Meanwhile, William couldn't even reload his rifle under pressure.

It was time to head home. Past time, in fact, but since he couldn't turn back the clock, he would leave now... or as quickly as he could without facing a backlash from these stirred-up, want-to-be killers.

As William was thinking these things and assuming he was alone in his opinions, Ethan said, "We're in trouble."

"Yeah," another guy who William didn't know agreed, nodding with haunted eyes. "They're going to come for us now. We best get out of here."

"What are you talking about?" Jem Pulcher sneered. "We hurt them, ran them off. This was a victory. Mr. Dumay is gonna be happy."

"Yeah," Post said. "Now they know we mean business. Didn't you see them run? They're finished."

Garrett slung his rifle over his shoulder, shaking his head. "They ain't finished. Ethan's right. We're in trouble. These men got a lot of fight left in them. Trust me. This thing's just getting started."

"You're crazy," one of the laughers said. "You see them high-tail it out of here? Like a bunch of rabbits on horseback."

This got the laughers laughing again, but William noticed that most of the men weren't laughing, and noticed, too, that many of those not laughing were physically distancing themselves from the others.

He wondered if they were even aware that they were stepping away from Pulcher and his trigger-happy idiots, who continued to recount their exploits.

Then someone pointed to the north and shouted, "Riders!"

William's guts turned to water again.

Heck Martin was coming for them!

Jem Pulcher spat, looking north to where the man was pointing. "I don't see nothing."

William stepped up beside them, pulled out his spyglasses, and scoped the country north of the trail, sweeping his magnified field of vision back and forth across the stony scrubland beyond the rutted expanse of the trail—and there they were, hurtling westward in a blur of movement.

"Two riders," William blurted.

Pulcher snatched the spyglasses from him. "Not two riders. Two horses. One rider. That's all I see. He leaned forward, studying the distant rider. That's the muleskinner, Burt Bickle."

"Shoot him," someone suggested.

"He's too far off, stupid," Post said, and cuffed the man.

"Far off and riding fast," Pulcher said. When he dropped the spyglasses, his eyes were narrowed with thought. "Bickle must be carrying something to Laramie. A message, something. We have to stop him."

"Let's go, then," Post said.

"No," Pulcher said. "Not all of us. Dumay will want a report, and we're getting more shorthanded everyday with cowards deserting. I need two volunteers to go stop him."

William and Ethan exchanged meaningful looks. And just like that, William knew he wouldn't be heading to California alone.

"I'll go," Post said.

"Me, too," another mean-looking man said.

"All right," Pulcher said. "You boys stop him however you can."

"He's riding awful fast," someone said.

"Slow and steady wins the race," Post countered. "We'll ride up there, find his tracks, and catch up with him tonight."

"How are you gonna track him in the dark, genius?"

"Well, I'm just saying we could ride longer than him."

While these men squabbled over the particulars, William grew more and more certain that he'd attached himself to a company of fools.

"Boss ain't gonna be happy about this," Jem Pulcher said. "He said don't let nobody through. Nobody. You boys get after Burt."

"What's Dumay gonna do, fire us?" Garrett asked. "I got half a mind to head home anyway. I got a bad feeling about this."

For a moment, no one said anything. Garrett was a big man, stronger than most, and his words had apparently struck the others in a way William's never would have.

William looked around the group, noting which men looked like they were commiserating with the notion.

"That's enough with that claptrap," Jem Pulcher said. "Post and Vincent, what are you still doing here? Go get him."

Post and Vincent shrugged and took their time gathering their things.

"We gotta head back to camp and let the boss know what happened," Jem Pulcher said.

Everything had changed again, William noted. No one was laughing or celebrating. A blanket of foreboding had settled over everyone, even the combative idiots.

"Why don't we just forget the rider and all head back?" someone said.

"Not a chance," Pulcher said. "What if that rider ends up causing trouble down the line, and Dumay figures out we let him escape?"

"You're afraid of Dumay?" Garrett snorted.

"I'm not afraid of Dumay one bit," Pulcher said, "but that Wedge, he's a stone-cold killer."

With the mention of Dumay's assassin, the sweat covering William's body iced over.

That was it. He had to get out of here. He wouldn't stay for another night.

But he couldn't go alone. He might get lost or run into Indians or get injured and need help.

At least there would be safety in numbers.

"Ethan," he called as the men started to mount up. "Garrett."

Both men turned toward him, and he could see in their eyes that they already knew what he was going to propose—and would be riding out of here with him.

The only question remaining was how many others could they sway into leaving with them?

CHAPTER 29

Heck sat atop a log to one side of the group, balancing Tor on his knee and listening to folks talk.

Hope couldn't join the town meeting because she was busy helping Doc take care of Maguire, who was having a hard day, and Derry, who'd gotten banged up in the stampede.

Folks had been talking—and shouting—for quite a while.

Heck had mostly listened, letting the others have their say.

All of them were angry. Dumay's brazen attack was an outrage. His men had shot Abe, tried to shoot the others, killed several steers, and scattered dozens more... many of which Dumay's miners had likely already captured for their own use.

Dumay had assaulted Heck's people, attempted murder, and slaughtered and rustled his livestock.

So yes, folks were angry. And desperate.

It was the ways in which they felt desperate that separated them.

Some were desperate to make peace. A few talked of leaving the valley. Others wanted to bargain with Dumay.

On the opposite end of things, some folks were desperate to fight. Several demanded war. They were tired of waiting. They wanted to mount up and attack Dumay—now.

Outspoken among this latter group was Heck's little brother, Seeker.

"We have to hit them," Seeker said, standing up to make his point.

Even though Heck disagreed with Seeker, he was proud of him. He wasn't just going to grow into a good man. He was going to become a good leader of men.

Here and there across the assembly, folks nodded. Seeker had proven himself over and over, and he held powerful sway in matters of violence.

"We can't let them get away with this," Seeker continued, staring across the group at Heck. "They're testing us. That's what this was, a test. If we don't hit them back, they're going to hit us harder. It's the way this sort of thing works."

"You have a point, little brother," Heck said, speaking up at last, "but you're giving Dumay too much credit. What you're describing, that's the way an Indian wages war."

"It's the way someone smart wages war," Seeker said.

"All right," Heck said. "But that's the thing. I don't think Dumay's all that smart, not in the ways of war. He's squandering his big advantage. If you were him, you would've ridden in here on day one, hard, and taken the fort while your men still had fighting spirit and you still had a big numerical advantage. But he didn't do that. Why?"

"He's worried we might whip him."

"Maybe. But I think he's worried about his reputation, as I've been saying."

"Some reputation," A.J. Plum said, "shooting cows."

Tor was getting fussy, so Heck pulled him off his knee and held him close.

"Things like that, shooting cows, stampeding them," Heck said, "they won't stick to his reputation, not really, and they sure won't make it all the way back to the West Coast. If he wipes out a town full of men, women, and children, though, that's a story that would travel far and wide."

"If he's so worried about his reputation, maybe we can do what we want," the Widow said. "I'm with Seeker. I say we attack."

More folks were nodding now.

Heck frowned. He knew the Widow's words carried weight.

"Look," he said, "I understand how you feel. I'd like nothing more than to pay them back and drive them out. But we can't let our anger blind us. Because no matter how justified that anger is, the truth remains the same. We cannot afford an all-out war with these people."

"We can whip them, Heck!" Seeker said.

"At what cost, little brother? There are too many of them, and we are too vulnerable. We need to keep breaking them down, but we can't stir them up so much they ride in here, blasting away."

"I reckon Heck's got a point," Ray McLean, the Australian mechanical genius and women's magazine editor said. "They don't belong here. They can't be happy. We ought to just keep whittling away at them."

"How?" Seeker said. "You people keep talking about breaking them, but they're still here."

"Not as many as there used to be," Heck pointed out.

"Yeah," Seeker said, "but according to you, there are still too many to fight."

"That's true. It wouldn't take too many of them to pin us down from uphill. Then the others could charge in here."

"We could hold the fort."

"Maybe. Depends on how many would be up on the slope above us, shooting down. Meanwhile, a bunch of them could ride through and burn Hope City. We have to keep fighting the way we've been fighting and wear them down."

"What, with signs and spreading rumors?" Seeker said, sounding disgusted. "That stuff isn't working."

"Oh, it's working," Heck said. "Some of them have been leaving."

"How many? Five? Ten?"

"More than that," Paul Wolfe spoke up, surprising Heck because the boy didn't usually speak in front of big groups, let alone to voice opposition to his mother and his best friend, Seeker. "I've been counting for a while now. Every time we go scouting, I count how many I can see. Granted, I can't see them all. But the thing is, the number keeps getting smaller. I'll bet twenty or thirty of them have left. Maybe more."

A hushed murmur went through the crowd.

The corners of the Widow's mouth curled almost imperceptibly upward. The woman was clearly proud of her son for speaking up and making a reasonable point, even though in doing so, he had contradicted her.

"Whatever the actual number," Heck said, "these tactics are

working. The longer we can stretch this thing out, the better. Nights will be getting colder. And for everyone who's left, a bunch more are thinking of leaving. We want to help them make that decision."

"Heck makes good sense," Titus said, rising from his seat and looking around the group, looking very much like a former cavalry officer. "Dumay is faced with a crisis of leadership. If more of his soldiers break ranks, many more will follow. That is our best weapon now, the enemy's flagging morale."

"I'm tired of waiting for them," Seeker said. "I want to do something." He turned to Heck. "Let me ride to the western mountains. I'll ask my uncle for help."

"No," Heck said. "The Shoshones can't help us. They signed the Horse Creek Treaty. They can't risk breaking it."

"Black Cloud is my uncle!" Seeker shouted. Heck had never seen the boy so upset. "My *real* uncle. Blood is stronger than any treaty!"

"Maybe so," Heck said, keeping his voice level, "but would you really do that to your uncle? Would you ask him to choose between loyalty to family and what's best for his people?"

Seeker turned sharply and stormed off.

Heck felt a stab of regret, wishing they hadn't aired their differences publicly, but there was nothing he could do about it.

"Seeker's right about one thing," Heck said. "We do have to respond. We do have to act now. Here's what I think we should do next..."

CHAPTER 30

Burt Bickle traveled fifty miles the first day, switching horses every hour until dark, when he broke and made camp without a fire, reckoning some of Dumay's men had probably spotted and followed him.

In country like this, fire was a welcome friend. It kept you warm, cooked your food, and kept the wolves at bay.

But you could see it from a long way off, and it served as a beacon for wolves of the two-legged variety.

So he ate a dinner of jerky and bread, washing it down with water, and was just getting ready to turn in when he spotted a point of light in the distance.

Against the absolute darkness, the faint light twinkled like a far-off star.

Burt opened his bag and pulled out his telescope and pointed it eastward, scanning his back trail until he found the light and drew it in.

As he had expected, the light wasn't actually twinkling. It was flickering.

He was too far away to make out any detail, but he could tell it was a campfire.

He hadn't passed anybody coming this way, so this had to be someone coming eastward at a clip, and the only people who would do that were Dumay's thugs.

How many were chasing him?

There was no way to tell from this distance, but even if there was only one of them, he didn't want anybody on his trail. That was a good way to get killed either going to Fort Laramie or coming back, and Burt had too much to live for to hand his life over to a bunch of back-shooting snakes like the ones who'd ambushed them this morning.

During the long ride, he'd gone back over the ambush many times, looking for what he might have done differently. But after all that thinking, he was convinced that there had been no way to anticipate or avoid the attack.

That was the advantage to a well-planned ambush, of course. All you had to do was sit back and wait for your clueless victims to come riding into the kill zone.

And Dumay's men had clearly known they were coming. That was another thing that had passed through his mind again and again over the course of the long ride, growing clearer and clearer with each reconsideration, until he was completely convinced that Dumay had been watching their every move, or, even more likely, had a spy in Hope City reporting their intentions.

He ran over everyone he could think of, trying to sort out a list of potential spies, but even after fifty miles, that list remained empty. Perhaps because his own mind was so honest and straightforward, he couldn't even conceive of anyone he knew perpetrating such unthinkable betrayal.

But over the course of all this riding and thinking, he had also come to a far more encouraging conclusion, a conclusion that steeled him now, emboldening him and sparking ideas that would not normally occur to him in a situation like this, with an unknown number of murderers chasing him across the wasteland.

Dumay's men couldn't fight. That was his conclusion. They had known Burt and his men were coming, had set up everything perfectly, and there had been at least a dozen of them firing at will—and yet, what had they accomplished?

If Heck had organized such an ambush with even half that number of men, Burt and everyone else would be dead, and Heck would have spared the steers and captured all two hundred and fifty of them for his own use.

But of course, Heck wouldn't do that. Because he wasn't a scoundrel like whoever was chasing after Burt now.

They'd had their shot and they'd taken it, poking a hole through Burt's shirt, grazing Abe, and badly injuring Derry, not to mention killing and scattering cattle.

Which again was bad—but downright pitiful considering the perfect ambush Burt had ridden into.

The more Burt thought about it, the more anger and contempt he felt toward them.

How dare they shoot at him? How dare they hurt his friends? How dare they kill and rustle Heck's cattle?

And now here they were, bumbling across the land, meaning to stop him and steal everything he had, including his life.

Of that, he was certain. These men were evil. They had proven that this morning.

Burt, on the other hand, was a man of character and experience. After years of delivering freight across dangerous and uncertain trails and all sorts of country, he was adaptable in the extreme, a decisive man of action accustomed to weighing risks and rewards and accustomed, also, to traveling by night, even through pitch darkness like this.

His eyes functioned well at night, and he knew enough to trust a horse and take cues from it while traveling through darkness. He had an unparalleled sense of direction, a good memory for trails he covered, a good feel for land, and knew how to navigate by the stars.

In other words, darkness to him was merely an inconvenience. It slowed him. That was all.

If he left now, he could easily put ten miles between himself and his pursuers by the time they woke the next morning.

He spoke softly to his horses then mounted up. But he left Derry's gelding hitched alongside his dry camp here at the edge of the trail.

Because he wasn't going to ride east and stretch out his lead, not without taking a closer look at his bumbling foes.

Burt rode west toward the flickering light and the would-be murderers gathered around it.

He pictured them sprawled around the fire, complaining about sore butts and backs, because he was certain that none of them, no matter how many they numbered, were conditioned to travel like he'd shown them today. He had pushed hard even for a freighter.

Burt rode slowly through the night, moving as safely and

silently as possible toward the light of the fire, which seemed to be dimming even as it drew closer.

They had probably already stretched out and gone to sleep, worn out by their big day ambushing him and giving chase.

He hoped pursuit had been an afterthought. If so, they had traveled without bedrolls and were sleeping on the hard ground.

Drawing closer, he swung to the southern edge of the trail, as it seemed they'd made their camp on the opposite side, a quarter of a mile away.

When he'd drawn even with their position, hitched his horse to a trailside rock, keeping the lead loose, enough so the horse would understand Burt wanted him to stay put but loose enough that Burt could untie him quickly and, if anything happened to Burt, the horse could pull free and run for home.

Not that Burt expected it to come to that. Otherwise, he wouldn't be here, moving through the darkness toward the enemy camp.

To save his night vision, he avoided looking directly at the campfire, which was guttering low now.

He doubted the men had even bothered to put out a guard, but he kept his rifle at the ready in case he was wrong.

Drawing closer to the camp, he saw that he was right. No guards. Just two lumps on the ground close to the campfire and further back, a pair of horses hitched there.

He carefully lowered the hammer on his rifle, slung it over his back with the strap running across his chest, and pulled his .36 caliber Colt 1851 Navy revolver, creeping closer and watching the lumps for any sign of movement as he circled in the outer darkness.

There was no movement, and as he came closer still, he heard one of the men snoring loudly.

They were out cold, sleeping with their feet to the flames.

In the flickering light of the dying fire, he saw their faces, the mustaches, their red shirts.

Yes, these were Dumay's men. These were the ones who'd shot at him and hurt his friends and killed Heck's cattle.

They were here for him, to kill and rob him, to stop him from completing his mission.

Lying there, slumbering deeply with exhaustion, mouths ajar, they looked like dead men—and he realized now, standing twenty feet behind them with his six-shooter at the ready, he could make them just that in a matter of just a few seconds.

Two pulls of the trigger would probably do it, but Burt prided himself on always doing a good job. He would unload all six rounds, reload, and give them another six.

If, that was, he decided to kill them in their sleep.

He was no stranger to violence. He'd battled bandits and Indians alike, and he'd killed several men.

But unlike these men, he was no murderer.

Yes, they deserved death for what they had done and what they were planning to do, but he would not kill them in their sleep.

If they woke and went for their guns, yes, he would finish them, but he wouldn't shoot sleeping men.

Training his pistol on them, he tiptoed forward.

Beneath the snoring of the loud man, he heard quieter snoring from the other.

Burt grinned and crept closer still until he was looming directly behind them.

It was tempting to wake them, fool them into going for their guns, and plug them both, but that wouldn't be much better than killing them in their sleep, and he certainly didn't want to take them prisoner.

What he wanted he crouched down and took, picking up one at a time and then coming back until all four were tied together and slung over the back of one of the horses.

Then he unhitched the horses. Taking the reins of one in his hand, he mounted the other horse and rode off toward his own steed.

Reaching that spot, he switched to his own horse and trailing the other two horses, swung back past the camp, not getting too close this time.

He grinned down at the saddle scabbards, which each held a rifle. He also had the men's boots, of course, and each had left his bags on his horse.

They had probably been too tired to care for the poor animals or even unpack their war bags.

Chuckling to himself, Burt fired a shot into the campfire, spraying sparks.

The men came awake, screaming their surprise and, unable to see him, peppered the surrounding darkness with pistol rounds.

That's it, he thought, *waste your ammunition.*

Each man shot a few times. Then they were up and scrambling around, shouting that someone had stolen their horses.

"Where are my boots?" one of them bellowed.

From a distance of seventy yards, Burt fired over their heads, causing both men to hit the dirt and fire wildly again.

"Have fun walking fifty miles back to camp with no boots," Burt hollered back at them.

They shouted curses, demanding he bring their things back. One of the men fired again, but the other abstained, probably realizing he was stuck in the middle of nowhere with no horse, no rifle, no boots, and only a round or two in his pistol.

Drifting away through the darkness, Burt laughed and hollered back one more time before abandoning them to the wilderness and the will of God. "You boys should've known better than to try and stop me. Bickle Freighting finds a way!"

CHAPTER 31

A few hours after Burt stranded his would-be murderers in the middle of nowhere, Heck and half a dozen hand-picked fighters crept silently through the forest and took up their positions behind the big pile of boulders where the valley floor met the edge of the forested slope.

On the other side of these boulders, Dumay's men had set up their sloppy watch, just as they had every night.

Tonight, however, there were only three of them. Normally, there were four.

What did that mean?

Had one of them left? Or was Dumay running a smaller crew because he had fewer men?

Heck waited for a while in case another man might be joining them, but none did.

These men were clearly not Indian fighters. They sat there, ignoring the surrounding darkness, staring into the flames, and talking loudly.

"Garrett, too?" one of them said.

"Yup. And Ethan."

"William and Ethan don't surprise me. In fact, it's a wonder they didn't desert on the way here. But Garrett seemed tough."

"Leaving doesn't make him weak," one of them said. "It makes him smart."

"Stow that talk, Cooper. If Wedge hears you…"

"Wedge won't hear me. What do you think, he's creeping around in the darkness like the bogeyman?"

"Not a chance. Dumay keeps him close in case Heck Martin shows up."

"Can you blame him? I wouldn't want Martin after me."

"Better Martin than Wedge. He's the deadliest man to ever walk the Earth."

"I don't know about that, but he'll kill Heck Martin, that's for sure."

Seeker grinned at Heck, the crescent of his bright teeth like a curved blade in the night.

"Well, I don't blame them for leaving," one of Dumay's sentries confessed. "I'm sick of this place. Sick to death of it."

"At least we got some beef."

"Yeah, but I'm tired of packing into the longhouse with everybody, smelling them."

"Pitch a tent."

"Getting cold. That's another thing. What's gonna happen when winter comes? I have half a mind to head west myself."

"Not me. I want that bonus."

"Five hundred dollars is a lot of money."

"More money than I've ever seen."

"I think I'd rather cut out now and live to spend what I've already got."

"You'd blow through it all in a week at the bars and bordellos."

"Maybe, but it'd be the best week of my life."

The men laughed.

Heck gestured to his fighters and moved.

Heck stepped around the boulder and put his Colt on the chuckling trio. "Hands up. That's it. Over your heads."

He didn't even need to threaten them. They complied immediately. Their huge eyes flashed in the firelight.

Paul disarmed the guards, while Heck's other men kept them covered from various angles—and kept an eye and an ear on the surrounding darkness.

Seeker remained out of sight, as planned.

"We didn't mean no harm, Mr. Martin," one of Dumay's men said.

"Yeah, we're just watching the cows is all," another said.

"Quiet," Shorty Potter said, and prodded the back of the last speaker's head with his scattergun.

"Seeker," Heck called. "They're ready for you."

Seeker came around the boulder slowly, his dark eyes gleaming like chips of wet obsidian in the flickering illumination of the fire. Below, the scimitar smile twisted cruelly upward as Seeker drew the long, heavy blade of his Bowie, letting it flash in the firelight.

"Hey now!" one of the men blurted. "What's he doing?"

Shorty prodded him with the shotgun. "Quiet."

One of Dumay's men set to mumbling prayers. Another could only weep.

The third man fell on his knees before Heck. "Mercy, Mr. Martin. We didn't do nothing."

"Mercy?" Heck said. "Like you showed my cattle?"

"That wasn't us, Mr. Martin! That was Pulcher and the others."

"Jem Pulcher?" Heck asked, the heat of anger warming his face.

"Yes, sir. He led the ambush."

Pulcher would pay. Heck would see to that. But Heck said, "You men should have left. You should have gone west while you still could."

"Too late now," Seeker said and took a step forward with his big, flashing blade.

"Wait!" the man on his knees begged. "It's not too late. We'll leave. Tonight."

"They're lying, Heck," Seeker said, sticking to the script he and Heck had devised before leaving the fort. "If we let them go, they'll just pretend to leave, then they'll head back to Dumay."

"Yeah," Shorty said. "Let's take care of them right now."

"No," the man on his knees insisted. "We won't come back. You'll never see us again. We'll leave straight from here and won't even go back to camp for our stuff. Isn't that right, boys?"

The other two nodded enthusiastically.

"You," Heck said, pointing to the one who had been praying. "Your prayers have saved you."

The man spilled forward with relief and cried out his thanks.

"Don't be thanking me. Thank the Lord I didn't let Seeker have his way with you. Now, can any of you write?"

The weeper wiped his eyes and raised a hand. "I can, sir."

"Excellent. What's your name?"

"Gerald, sir."

"All right, Gerald. Paul, give him the pen and paper. Gerald, you're going to write what I tell you. Nothing more, nothing less. Understand?"

"Yes, sir."

"I like your attitude, Gerald. That's exactly the sort of attitude that will help you boys survive."

Paul handed Gerald the pen and paper, and Gerald flattened it against a saddle bag and wrote exactly what Heck told him to write.

"Perfect," Heck said. "Set it there, where Dumay's men will be sure to see it. Weigh down the corners with small stones. That's it. I don't want the wind blowing it away. Your buddies need to read this. All right. Seeker, Paul, check their bags. Confiscate any weapons but leave food, pictures, stuff like that."

The boys went to work, capturing a pistol, a few knives, and a hatchet, all of which they stowed on the men's horses, which Heck was also taking.

"All right," Heck said to the prisoners. "Come on with us now."

"Where? You ain't gonna shoot us, are you?"

"Shoot you?" Heck said, letting amusement show in his voice. "Not unless you give us trouble. You boys mind your manners, we'll give you some food to carry out of here. It's a long way back to California. Might even have some pie for you."

"Pie?" Gerald said, his eyes lighting up so brightly that Heck wondered if Hope and her mother could put down Dumay's whole army with a few wagonloads of baked goods.

"That's right, pie," Heck said, knowing that kindness alone would never actually be enough to repel these thugs. Some men, having lived rough and violent lives, only listened if they feared you. "But if you boys ever come back to this valley, we'll turn *you* into mincemeat."

The men assured Heck they would never return. Believing them, he drove them northward, where he would, of course, make good on his promises and send them on their way with enough food to give them a chance of surviving.

Behind them, the wind continued to blow, shaking but not dislodging Gerald's note to those who remained with Dumay.

CHAPTER 32

Percival Dumay awoke feeling triumphant. Now, seated at his desk before a plate of bacon, toast, and hot cakes, his sense of triumph increased. Nearly all was right in the world.

Yes, a proper breakfast would include eggs, but Wyatt swore Heck Martin had chickens. Soon enough, Dumay would have eggs again.

Everything was going his way at last.

The only damper on the moment was Frank Wedge, who leaned beside the door, looking bored and malicious and somehow contemptuous, as usual.

"Why the long face, Mr. Wedge?" Dumay asked. "We've driven back their cattle, wounded their men, and shown them we mean business. By now, our men will have stopped their messenger. Meanwhile, my own messengers will have already reached Fort Laramie. Before long, the cavalry will arrive and deal with these vermin. The valley is mine. All I have to do is wait!"

"This valley won't be yours until Heck Martin is dead," Wedge said. "Mark my words. He will fight until the end."

"Not when my plan comes to fruition. Heck Martin will be powerless. And that will be that. He'll limp off, ruined and humiliated."

Wedge shook his head. "He'll fight."

"Against the army?"

"Against anybody."

Dumay chuckled. Now, it was his turn to feel contempt. Wedge clearly had far too much faith in Heck Martin. "If he fights the army, they'll wipe him out."

"How many are they sending?"

"I don't know. It doesn't matter."

"Oh, it matters all right."

Dumay shook his head and skewered a half-strip of bacon with his fork. "If he resists the soldiers, they'll send more."

"And before they get here, you'll be dead."

"Not with you as my bodyguard."

Wedge spread his hands. "I'm only one man."

"Are you saying you can't handle him?"

"Not at all. If he comes a knockin', I'll put him in the ground. But what if you call in the army, and he beats them back, and finally decides he's done fooling around and sets up in those woods a couple hundred yards to the east? How am I supposed to stop him if he decides to put a bullet through your chest at that distance?"

"He wouldn't do that."

"How do you know that? How much do you really know about Heck Martin? See, I've known men like him. And I'm telling you, he will never tuck his tail and go out with his head hung low. Never. If he realizes his power's running out, he'll come at us with everything he's got, head held high, guns blazing."

"I don't believe that for one moment. He's young and has a wife and child, not to mention a boxing title and a sizable fortune. He'd never risk all that for this valley, especially when he's outgunned."

"You're wrong, boss. If he was the sort of man you're counting on him to be, he wouldn't have everything you just mentioned. You know where he's from, don't you?"

"Originally?"

Wedge nodded.

Dumay thought for a moment, which was inconvenient when all he wanted to do was wallow in his impending victory. "Somewhere back east. Kentucky, right?"

"Not just Kentucky. The mountains."

"And?"

"Have you ever been back in those mountains?"

"Thankfully, no."

"Folks are different back there. You might even say they're peculiar. See, those mountaineers, most of them have never had any money nor any way to make it. They're poor as dirt and proud of it. But they all seem to have three things. You know what three things they have?"

"I have no idea."

"Mountaineers have land, guns, and tempers like hornets in July. You cross them, they call it a feud, and the next thing you know, you are eyeballs deep in blood. All of them, the whole clan, young and old, fight to the bitter end. Once offended, they are the most combative people in the world."

"Well, we're not facing a whole clan, merely one Kentuckian and a few of his friends."

"A man like Heck Martin, he affects people."

"He certainly seems to be affecting you."

"Only a fool disregards the strengths of his enemies. You need to understand who you're up against. From what I hear, Heck Martin left home four years ago with nothing. He's an orphan."

"Stop," Dumay said flatly, his voice thick with sarcasm. "You're breaking my heart."

Wedge ignored him. "Now look at him. He owns this whole valley and has a town of folks depending on him. He's already won a boxing title and earned a fortune. He's killed dozens of men—not to mention a few grizzly bears, at least one of which he finished with his Bowie knife. Apparently, he speaks several languages and reads them, too. Not just Indian languages. French, Spanish, German, Latin."

Dumay rolled his eyes. Why was Wedge being so tiresome this morning? It was ruining Dumay's mood and his appetite. He laid his fork and uneaten bacon on the plate. "That doesn't matter here."

"Oh, it could matter. Point is, he's not just tough. He's smart, too. And if the army doesn't finish the job, he will come for you."

Dumay blinked at him. Suddenly, his face felt very hot. "I'm not worried," he lied.

"You should be. Now is the time, before it's too late. Let me call him out, and I will kill him for you."

Dumay shook his head. "What a brash, foolish move that

would be. The army could be here any day, any hour. We will let them handle Martin for us."

Wedge frowned.

Dumay picked up his fork again and took a bite of the bacon. "You seem to enjoy talking about this hard world and all these unsavory characters you know, Mr. Wedge. But in my world, the world that matters, this is how you do things. You stand back and let the authorities handle problems. Then, when the dust settles, your trouble is over, and your reputation is intact."

Wedge shook his head, visibly irritated for the first time. "You keep telling yourself that, and you'll be taking that reputation straight to the grave. Why don't you let me—"

They were interrupted by a knock at the door. Wedge opened it.

A frazzled messenger entered. "They're gone, sir."

"Who's gone?"

"The cattle guards. The night watch, I mean. Me and the others went to relieve them, but they're gone."

"Where did they go?" Wedge asked.

"Deserted, sir."

"What?" Dumay snapped, irritation rising in him, ruining his mood completely. More deserters? Why were so many men leaving? He was offering an unspeakably generous bonus. "Are you certain?"

"Yes, sir. I'm certain they deserted." He held out a piece of paper. "They left this note. Everybody in camp is all up in arms about it."

Dumay snatched the note from the man's hand and read it.

We're done here. We don't have anything against these people and don't like what Dumay is doing. He's fixing to get everyone killed. So the three of us hereby resign. If you're reading this, you should leave, too, because if you stay, you are going to die.

CHAPTER 33

Major Avery Scottsdale, West Point graduate and career soldier, was a man of duty—but also a man of honor. And in this moment, those two ideals were in direct conflict.

The mission he'd been tasked to supply was wrong. Avery was sure of it.

Of course, down through history, across the world, how many soldiers had carried on despite questioning their mission?

All of them. At least all of them worth remembering.

Army life could be very difficult at times. Nothing was harder, however, than operating under unethical orders.

But Avery was a man of duty first and honor second, and yes, he would do his duty… eventually.

So he busied himself with other matters for days until, at last, Colonel Harper summoned him once more.

With great trepidation, Avery reported to his commander

and confessed that he still had not prepared the supplies for Sergeant Earl's expedition to Heck's Valley.

He gave no specific reason for this and was relieved when Colonel Harper did not ask for one.

"That is an unfortunate delay, Major," Colonel Harper said with just the hint of a smile. "These sorts of problems arise from time to time, of course. Such a delay might even hold the men up for a few more days. I will adjust my expectations."

"Very well, sir," Avery said, keeping a straight face despite feeling a powerful surge of relief and hope.

Harper's smile flattened. "But then, I expect those men to be on the road. Do I make myself clear?"

"Yes, sir."

Harper leaned back, shaking his head. "I don't like this situation any better than you do, Major, but General Bradbury can be a brutally vindictive man. I will not endanger my career for Heck Martin."

"No, sir. Of course not, sir."

"Good. I'm glad we understand one another. You're a good man, Major, but don't let that stand in the way of doing what's right."

"Sir?"

"Heck Martin is larger than life, a frontier legend in the making."

"It's all true, sir. Everything people say about him. I knew him back at Fort Bent, when he was trapping with Kit Carson, Jim Bridger, and the other mountain men. Why, one winter, I swear we would have starved if it wasn't for Heck. He—"

"I know it's all true, Major. He is the genuine article. The trouble with a man like Heck Martin is that he does not fit within society. He's too big, too strong, and, if you'll forgive me for waxing philosophical, too ethical. Sooner or later, a man like Heck Martin ends up standing in the way of society—or, more precisely, standing in the way of those who run it."

"Men like General Bradbury."

"I didn't say that, Major, but I see you understand my point. Unfortunately, society has limited ways of coping with men like Heck Martin. Limited yet highly effective. Prisons and the gallows come to mind."

Avery shook his head, knowing his commanding officer was right and hating that truth.

"So no, I don't like this mission any more than you do. But as your superior officer, I feel the need to offer a warning."

"Yes, sir?"

"Men like Heck Martin possess great magnetism. And it is easy for men like us, men of ideals, to be swayed by men like Heck Martin."

"Yes, sir."

"I've already told you I won't sacrifice my career for this legend in the making. I suggest you make a similar pledge to yourself and your career, Major, before it's too late."

"Yes, sir."

"See that those men are on the road no later than Saturday."

"Yes, sir."

Harper dismissed him but called again, stopping Avery in the doorway.

"Yes, sir?"

"Who knows, Major? Perhaps this unfortunate delay will give your friend a chance to deal with this situation so we don't have to." Harper offered a wry smile. "That would certainly enlarge that legend of his, eh?"

"Yes, sir. It certainly would."

Cutting across the courtyard, Avery thanked God for his exchange with Colonel Harper.

Harper was not angry with him. If anything, he seemed pleased. But he had also made it clear that the expedition would leave no later than Saturday.

Saturday, then. And not a moment sooner.

Yes, this would buy Heck a few more days. Hopefully, Heck understood the situation and would take this opportunity to resolve it.

In the meantime, Avery's mind raced.

There had to be some way to help Heck. That's what he'd been doing, of course, by delaying things, but it wasn't enough.

Once again, he found himself at the crossroads of duty and doing what was right. Presently, those two paths shot off in opposite directions.

How could he help Heck? And more importantly, how could he help Heck without disobeying direct orders?

He could think of nothing. This was a miserable dilemma.

Perhaps he had done all he could for his old friend. Perhaps there was nothing else to—

"Major Scottsdale?" a voice called.

Avery turned and saw an exhausted-looking man covered in trail dust coming his way. "Yes, I'm Major Scottsdale."

The man came shakily to attention and offered a weary salute, and a bright smile split his filthy face.

Only then did Avery recognize him. "My apologies, Mr.

Bickle. I didn't recognize you for a moment. If you don't mind my saying so, you look rather ragged."

Burt Bickle's chin lifted a little. "I should, sir. After all, I've ridden two hundred miles in three days."

"Two hundred miles in three days?" Avery said, not bothering to disguise his dismay.

"That's right, sir. Heck Martin sent me. He needs you, sir."

CHAPTER 34

Hig, atop the ridge overlooking the southern valley, Heck and Seeker watched the lone rider pause and glance back toward Dumay's camp.

Studying the man's face in the spyglasses, Heck said, "He's not up to any trick. He's running out. I can see it in his face, the way he's moving, everything. He's frightened."

"Good," Seeker said as the man down in the field turned west again and spurred his horse. "Him leaving will save a bullet."

Though, come to think of it, Heck doubted very much that the man owned his steed. He was stealing it from Dumay and making a break for freedom across a muddy trail that many others had clearly beaten into the ground.

Heck didn't know how many of Dumay's men had deserted, but it was a bunch. At least a dozen and probably two or three times that number.

Heck's tactics were working. By planting signs, leaving

letters, and spreading rumors through citizens of Hope City disguised as passing emigrants, he was weakening Dumay's men.

The cattle guards they'd captured and fed and sent off with sacks full of food had told tales of growing discontent, desertion, fear, and even insubordination.

Dumay rarely left his cabin and always kept Frank Wedge close.

The men resented this. They were sick of their horrible living conditions, tired of the same old trail food. They were worried. Worried about Heck, worried about Seeker, worried about starving or freezing or getting attacked by Indians.

Through the men's actions and stories, Heck had come to realize that Dumay's men felt no loyalty toward their employer.

They were henchmen, not friends. And that was an important distinction.

So Heck would continue whittling away at Dumay's force while doing his best to avoid a big battle.

Luckily, Dumay also seemed to want to avoid such a battle, probably to protect his reputation.

Dumay was thinking like a businessman. Heck's trading post business had dried up shortly after Dumay had arrived. Not a single emigrant had visited the trading post in several days, and Heck was convinced that Dumay had been stopping them and driving them off, just as he had turned Heck's cattle back.

In that sense, Dumay was thinking like a businessman, too. He knew the loss of cattle would hurt Heck and knew, somehow, that Heck didn't have enough grass on his own land to feed the big herd.

Thinking of Dumay's attack on the cattle, Heck couldn't help but wonder about Burt.

Knowing the freighter, he had already reached Fort Laramie and delivered Heck's message to Avery Scottsdale. Burt pushed himself hard and was unwaveringly dependable.

Still, it had been foolish for Burt to set off on his own across that country.

Heck sure hoped he was okay.

Derry had healed well, though his torso was bruised so spectacularly he could've starred in a sideshow and charged a nickel a head to see it.

Maguire, on the other hand, was still in rough shape. Even if he made a full recovery, the men who'd beat him had changed his life forever.

Maguire's face would be heavily scarred, and he was missing all his front teeth.

Doc said Maguire would have a pronounced limp for the rest of his life and doubted he would ever regain sight in his left eye, which would throw off a lot of his work as a cowboy if he was ever well enough to resume those duties again.

The big question was his insides. He was still passing blood, and his abdomen remained badly distended from whatever internal damage Dumay's thugs had done to the poor cowboy.

All they could do now was pray, keep working on the morale of Dumay's men, and hope that Burt had gotten through and that Avery Scottsdale would send some troopers to run off Dumay and his henchmen.

As these thoughts were running through Heck's mind, Seeker pointed. "Look."

The deserter had left the grassy field, following the muddy trail into the western woods.

But he'd only made it a short distance when four men jumped up, two on one side of the trail and two on the other. These men pointed their rifles at the man, who stopped his horse and held his hands in the air.

The shouting of the men who'd intercepted him floated faintly up to Heck and Seeker.

The shouting men pulled the would-be deserter off the horse and knocked him back and forth for a while, beating him with their fists and feet and the butts of their rifles.

Then they prodded him with their barrels and started marching him back across the field toward camp.

"He didn't make it too far," Seeker said.

"Nope. They were waiting for him. Or waiting for someone, anyway."

"Dumay probably has them watching the trail."

Heck nodded. "It's interesting. They're employees, not soldiers. How can he stop them from deserting?"

Seeker grinned. "I reckon we just saw exactly how he can stop them, big brother."

Heck laughed. "You're absolutely right. That's the trouble with holding individual liberty as sacred. It gives you blind spots because you forget, sometimes, that other men don't give a hoot about freedom."

They turned and rode across the ridge for miles until they came to its northern edge and were looking down on Dumay's other camp. Once more, they pulled out their spyglasses.

There was no comparison between this encampment of

stalled mining wagons and Dumay's main camp in the grassy valley. This camp was all lean-tos and squalor.

"That's strange," Seeker remarked.

"What's that?"

"Where are the oxen?"

Heck swept his glasses back and forth. "You're right. I don't see a single one."

"I'll bet Dumay has them all down there with him," Seeker said. "He's probably worried that if he leaves them here, these men will pull out and head for California."

"I wouldn't be surprised if they would," Heck said. "Dumay should have assigned good leaders here. Look how close they put their latrine."

Seeker shook his head in disgust. "Lazy. Must stink to high heaven down there."

Heck nodded. "They stay there, they're all gonna get sick."

"Good. I hope they all catch something and die."

"I'd rather see them leave."

Seeker shrugged. "Either way works. I just want them out of here. I want to get back to building our town, exploring caves, and running cattle."

"And getting ready for winter," Heck said. "Meanwhile, these boys don't look like they've made any provisions for winter whatsoever. They're sleeping in tents and stretching out their bedrolls beneath the wagons. You know what that means?"

"They're stupid?"

Heck chuckled. "Well, I won't argue that. But it also means they don't plan on sticking around here."

"You think they're planning on moving south?"

"I do."

"Which means they think they're coming down our road."

"That's right, little brother. No way they're getting those heavy wagons anywhere without a road. I shouldn't be surprised. It's exactly what Dumay said he would do on day one. He said he'd come down our road, take over the fort, and start mining. Apparently, he still expects that to happen."

"Well, he's in for a surprise."

"I happen to agree with you, but you always want to study your enemy. Sometimes, you can figure out what he's planning by things that don't even seem to play into it."

"Like the state of his camp?"

"That's right, little brother. Which tells us he still thinks he's bringing these men south—and soon."

"Because otherwise, they would be building cabins."

"That's right."

"But why does he think that?" Seeker asked. "Sure, he pushed our cattle back, but if you're right, and he doesn't want a battle, why would he think we would budge, especially when his men are leaving in droves?"

"Exactly. And I don't know the answer."

"Which means that's our vulnerability," Seeker said.

"That is correct, little brother. We need to figure out why Dumay is still so confident. He must have something up his sleeve. I just can't imagine what it would be. Whatever the case, I like the way you think. You keep ducking bullets long enough to grow up, you are going to become a formidable man."

Seeker stuck out his chest. "I already am a man. Let me prove it."

"What do you mean?"

"You know what I mean."

"You want to ride west and talk to your uncle?"

Seeker nodded. "Especially now with Dumay planning something we can't sort out. Heck, I really think my uncle will help us. He helped us against the Sioux. And the others will help, too. You gave them all those steers last fall. That meant a lot to the tribe. Besides, me and them, we're kin."

He nodded thoughtfully. "I just don't think they'll risk breaking the treaty."

"Well, there's only one way to find out," Seeker said. "If Black Cloud came back with even ten warriors, it could make a real difference."

Heck nodded, again impressed with Seeker's thinking. The boy sure had grown up since Heck first discovered him hiding in the root cellar.

"It'll be risky, riding alone," Heck said.

Seeker grinned. "Don't worry about me. I'm Seeker Yates, son of Badger Yates, nephew of Black Cloud, little brother to none other than the world-famous Heck Martin."

Heck laughed. "Yeah, well you just remember what I said about ducking bullets."

"So I can go?"

"Yes, you can go. You talked me into it. I doubt it'll work, but I appreciate that you're willing to face hardship and danger to save our valley."

"It ain't for the valley, Heck," Seeker said, and suddenly, he looked much older than his thirteen years. "It's for the people. It's for you and Hope and my nephew, Tor. It's for the Mullens and everybody else. You always say a man that isn't willing to protect the folks he loves is no man at all."

Heck smiled, surprised to feel a lump in his throat. "You are right, little brother. You are absolutely right."

"Great," Seeker said. "I'm gonna throw together a war bag, steal a slice of Hope's cake, and head for the hills."

"Good man," Heck said. "And hopefully while you're away, Avery Scottsdale will come riding in here with about a hundred cavalry troopers and drive Dumay out of the country."

"Now that, I'd like to see."

"Me, too. In the meantime, we'll keep chipping away at Dumay, see what happens, and hope our other friend arrives early."

"Other friend? Who's that?"

"Snow."

CHAPTER 35

D umay paced back and forth, considering the current
situation.

He'd been thinking about the army.

Where were they?

Surely, they should have been here already.

His riders had returned from Laramie and said the army
would be sending help.

So where was the cavalry?

Dumay had done everything correctly and paid a lot of
money to ensure success, but he knew better than to latch too
rigidly onto one plan.

It was a lesson business had taught him well, and he had
prospered not only by analyzing and planning but also by
thinking and acting decisively in the moment.

If the army did not come clean up this mess, he wasn't sure
what, exactly he would do, but—

There was a knock at the door.

Wedge came off the wall and pulled one of his pistols.

Outside, men were shouting.

Dumay blinked with dismay. What was going on? Had Heck Martin come for him?

It was a terrifying notion—but when Wedge opened the door, Dumay saw not Heck Martin by Jem Pulcher and several other men.

One of them sagged in the grip of two others. His face was lumped and bloody. He wept openly.

"What happened to this man?" Dumay demanded.

"Ran out on you," Jem said and cuffed the crying man in the back of the head. "Deserter."

Wedge shifted his gaze to Dumay. They had talked about this moment.

Dumay felt sick to his stomach. He knew what he had to say, what he had to do.

He was no savage, but here in this place, under these circumstances, he had to forget about who he had been and intended to be again—and for this brief, awful moment in time, become the person he must be to emerge from this crisis victorious.

"He stole your horse, too," Jem said.

Dumay latched onto that crime. Across the frontier, horse theft was a capital crime. Having caught this man in the act of stealing his horse, Dumay could easily justify—

But no.

The steady gaze of Wedge's pale blue eyes brought Dumay back to their conversation.

What happened now had to make a statement.

A specific statement.

It didn't matter if people agreed with his judgment. Only that they understood its message.

"Call the men together," Dumay said. "I want everyone to hear this."

Men went off to gather the others, but the command was unnecessary because they were already drifting toward the commotion.

Maybe Wedge was right. Maybe the men were waiting for this.

Dumay's gorge rose. He did not want to do this.

But he had to. He couldn't surrender, couldn't let Heck Martin win, couldn't let Heck Martin go unpunished for what he had done the day of the auction.

Remembering humiliation of that day, he was bolstered by fresh anger.

Yes, he had come all this way, gone to all this trouble. He couldn't fold now. He had to see this through.

Wedge was right.

So when the other men had gathered around, Dumay delivered the speech Wedge had recommended.

"This man betrayed us all. He deserted us here in our moment of need. We are all in this together. The enemy is watching us. The enemy will attack if they sense weakness. So this man, this *deserter*, put all of us in mortal danger."

He glanced around. Everyone was staring at him, waiting to see what would happen.

"I'm sorry," the deserter sobbed. "I won't do it again."

Dumay felt a stab of panic. He couldn't let the man talk, couldn't let him generate sympathy in the ranks.

Unable to help himself, Dumay blurted, "And he stole a horse."

He nodded to Wedge and pronounced, "I hereby sentence this deserter to death."

"Death?" a nearby man squawked. "You can't—"

The gunshot shattered his objection.

Wedge had his gun back in its holster before the man even hit the ground, shot through the heart and dead as a doornail.

The sound of the gunshot echoed up and down the valley then faded, leaving only silence and shocked expressions.

Horrified and sickened, Dumay did not let these things show. Instead, he gave the all-important announcement Wedge had suggested.

"The punishment for desertion is death!"

CHAPTER 36

Major Avery Scottsdale, having slept poorly since receiving Heck's letter, needed a change of scenery.

He had to get away from this office, away from the fort, away from all reminders of how he had failed his friend.

So he told Corporal Ennis that he was going to leave the fort and check the surrounding community of Laramie for any fortuitous arrival of goods.

"Want me to go with you, sir?" Corporal Ennis asked.

"That won't be necessary," Avery said. "This late in the season, I doubt there will be anything worth our while, but I need to check anyway."

And that was the truth, Avery realized as he left his office, not just an excuse to step away from the army for a moment.

This late in the season, it was unlikely that anything of real value would be arriving, but Fort Laramie and the ragtag town growing around it saw all sorts of traffic, not only passing emigrants, and one never knew when an Indian or mountain man might bring in a wagon of meat or a bundle of furs.

Of course, if that happened, the men at the gate would alert Avery, but it was good, occasionally, to show initiative, leave the fort, and walk among the transients.

Besides, someone traveling east might bring news of Heck and the horrible situation there.

For days, Avery had been pounding away at the same problem. How could he possibly help his friend while still doing his duty as an officer?

He had, of course, done his best to delay the expedition, but now they had left, and he felt hollowed out. The delay hadn't been enough.

He carried Heck's letter in his breast pocket, where it's unanswered plea sickened Avery's heart.

He couldn't help but remember the long, brutal winter when then Captain Avery Scottsdale had faced the very real possibility of starving his men.

Until, of course, a young Heck Martin had saved them all, braving deep snow and bitter cold on that huge red horse of his, venturing out into the frozen wasteland and coming back day after day with fresh meat when no one else could bag so much as a squirrel.

It was as if, Avery reflected now, God had blessed Heck above all others—and Heck had used that blessing to bless other people, keeping them alive and allowing a certain cavalry supply officer to rise through the ranks to a position of significance... which Avery now found utterly meaningless, as it had not allowed him to return such a primal favor.

He had to find a way, had to help Heck as Heck had helped him.

So he walked, happy to leave the fort, and drew his lungs full, breathing in through his nostrils and expanding his chest and holding onto the air before releasing it slowly and evenly.

Soon, he was striding along, blood pumping as he swung his arms and legs, feeling better. He shook off the paralysis and frustration of recent days, and the world around him came into clearer focus.

With summer having drawn to a close, Laramie no longer boiled with activity but merely simmered. Gone were the noise and trouble and expectations of the often ill-equipped and ill-fated emigrants.

Those left behind were made of harder stuff, mostly merchants who would either rush east or hunker down now to spend the winter in the shadow of the fort.

Indians were plentiful, too, of course, and with the disappearance of emigrants, Avery saw a larger number of hunters, trappers, and returning scouts.

Seeing them threw salt in the wound of his failure, because these men, who came and went as they pleased, completely outside of the military structure, reminded him of Heck Martin.

In fact, he realized, seeing a cluster of rough-looking men in buckskins, Heck probably knew most of them.

Which meant they knew Heck...

Feeling a surge of hope, Avery marched up to the group, which turned to him, their eyes full of the calculation and suspicion characteristic of their breed.

"Gentlemen," Avery said, "my name is Major Avery Scottsdale. I need to speak to you not as an officer but as a man."

They looked at him, saying nothing.

"A good friend of mine is in dire trouble, but there is nothing I can do... except tell you."

The men remained silent, their suspicious eyes narrowing further.

"His name is Heck Martin," Avery said.

And suddenly, everything changed.

"What's wrong with Heck?" one man demanded.

The others drew closer, wanting to know.

So Avery told them.

At first, he meant only to tell them the basics—an outsider was threatening Heck and the town he was carving out of the wilderness—but the more he talked, the more he told them, realizing they had to understand the full situation if they were really going to be able to help their mutual friend.

So he told them everything, ending his tale with, "He really needs your help."

Then, having done all that he could do, he awaited their response.

"Heck saved my life down on the Arkansas," one man said.

"Heck speak truth," an Indian observed. "Good man."

"He saved me from a bear attack," another man, whom Avery recognized as the traveling chronicler, added with enthusiasm. "Then his wife nursed me back to health."

The chronicler slapped his haversack. "Got it all written down here. I'll tell you the truth. Of all the men I've seen, of all the tales I've collected, of all the stories I've heard, none of them hold a candle to Heck Martin. If Heck's in trouble, I'm going to help him."

Every last one of them agreed. They were heading out immediately to help their friend—or, in the case of those few who had never met Heck, to help the man they'd heard so much about during their time on the wild frontier.

"Thank you," Avery said, feeling incredibly grateful to this group of rough-looking characters. "You'll have to hurry. The troop left this morning. You'll need to ride fast if you want to get there before them and help Heck before the cavalry arrives."

"Our friend is in trouble, Major," a scout said. "We'll ride like lightning."

"You got that right," said the oldest of the men, a familiar-looking, gray-bearded mountain man whose smell made Avery wince. "Why, Heck Martin is like a son to me!"

CHAPTER 37

"B urt," Heck said, cutting through the concerned people surrounding the freshly returned freighter.

Heck helped his clearly exhausted friend down from an equally exhausted horse.

Burt sagged against him, unable to stand on his own.

"Are you okay, Burt? What happened?"

Burt handed Heck an envelope. "I'm sorry, Heck. I rode night and day. I did everything I could. But the army can't help us."

Disappointment washed over Heck. He had hoped Avery might help.

"You did all you could and then some, Burt. Thank you. I can't believe you made it all the way there and back so quickly."

Burt nodded wearily. "Bickle Freighting finds a way."

"That is the truth if I have ever heard it spoken," Heck said and patted the man gently on the back. "Bickle Freighting finds a way. Doc, can you give Burt a hand?"

"Sure thing, Heck." Doc moved forward with his characteristic can-do attitude and helped Burt struggle toward his office, where Dusty Maguire still lay in a perilous state.

The citizens of Hope City followed Burt, asking questions.

Heck went in the opposite direction, wanting to read the letter from Avery Scottsdale.

———

DRAWN OUTSIDE BY THE COMMOTION, HOPE MET HER HUSBAND at the door.

She could see by his face that something was wrong. He carried something in his hand. It looked like an envelope.

Toddling along at her side, Tor saw his father and trundled excitedly forward, shouting, "Daddy!"

Heck crouched and spread his arms.

Tor charged straight into them.

Heck hugged the boy to his chest, and Tor laughed as Heck stood again, hoisting him high into the air.

Hope smiled, as she always did, to see her husband and son together. Nothing made her heart sing like seeing the two of them loving each other.

Even now, even with everything that was happening, the sight filled her with joy. It was, after all, nothing less than a dream come true. The only man she had ever loved being a great father to the son they had created together. Absentmindedly, she dropped a hand to her belly and their second child growing there.

But as Heck started toting their boy toward the cabin, she

saw something in her husband's blue eyes that reminded her that he bore bad news.

"What happened?" she asked.

"Burt's back."

That made no sense. Unless, she realized, Burt had been turned back before reaching Fort Laramie. She said as much.

"No," Heck said, smiling sadly. "He made it."

"That quickly?"

Heck nodded and held the cabin door for her. "That quickly. He's quite a man, our friend Burt Bickle. I don't know how he traveled four hundred miles in six days, but he and the horses are exhausted."

"I imagine," Hope said, feeling a surge of compassion for the heroic freighter and his horses. "What did he say?"

"The army can't help us."

Hope's mouth dropped open with shock and sudden anger. She felt like she'd been slapped in the face. "What? Why? They're going to let Dumay get away with this? I thought Avery Scottsdale was your friend."

"He is my friend. But he's also an army officer, so he can only do what he can do."

"Which is?"

"That's what I'm fixing to find out. Here, little man. Daddy's gotta set you down for a minute and read this letter."

Heck opened the envelope and read aloud, "Dear Heck, it is with the heaviest of hearts that I inform you, my friend, of the worst news possible."

Hope listened, her shock and anger growing as her husband continued to read the major's letter aloud.

Dumay had paid off politicians, who had granted him

timber rights on Heck's land and enlisted the help of a high-ranking army officer, who had commanded Fort Laramie to dispatch a sizeable troop of cavalrymen to settle matters in Heck's Valley. Not to set matters right, however. They had been ordered to clear a path for Dumay and to arrest Heck if necessary.

"Do not fight them, Heck," Heck read aloud. "I implore you not to fight them."

"I thought this man was your friend," Hope said. She was so angry she was trembling. "He has to know we'll fight. This is our land, not Dumay's and not the army's. They have no right to come here and do these things."

Heck nodded and held up a finger, wanting to share the rest of the letter.

Hope sat there, shaking with rage.

"If you are going to do anything to change this situation, you must act now. I will delay the men as long as I can, but by the time you receive this letter, they will already have left. They will reach you in a matter of days, not weeks. Good luck, old friend. Yours, Major Avery Scottsdale. P.S. Remember the Spartans."

Heck befuddled her then, chuckling. She understood it had something to do with the postscript and asked about it.

"The Spartans were a warrior culture in ancient Greece. They were very powerful despite the fact that they were always outnumbered. They fought in the most famous last stand in history, the battle of Thermopylae. Three hundred Spartans held back a million Persian invaders for three days while waiting for help to arrive."

Hope thought she understood now. "And on the third day, help arrived?"

Heck shook his head. "No. Help never arrived. All the Spartans died."

"That's horrible. Why would Major Scottsdale mention that?"

"Because he wants us to fight like lions, which we will. Besides, the Spartans might have died, but they bought time for the other Greeks to finally come to their senses. The death of the Spartans united the Greeks, and they went on to crush the Persians. That's why outnumbered soldiers still say, 'Remember the Spartans.'"

"Well, we're not hanging around waiting for help that will never arrive," Hope said.

"No," Heck said. "We need to go on the offensive and drive off Dumay before the cavalry arrives."

"But how can we do that? We're outnumbered."

"I've been working on a plan. It's a long shot, but if we pull it off, we might break them before the cavalry arrives."

"We should kill Dumay," Hope said. It wasn't like her to call down the death of a man, but Dumay was here to rob and kill everyone she loved, including her parents, brother, husband, and children. "The others wouldn't keep fighting without him, would they?"

Heck shook his head. "Not a chance. They're hirelings, not friends, family, or loyal followers. But we can't just kill Dumay."

"Why?"

"Well, I'd prefer to run him off, for starters. But we can't even do that. He's careful. He stays locked away behind the army with a professional killer at his side. I couldn't get within a hundred yards of him."

When Heck spoke these words, Hope's mind went to work. If not Heck…

As Hope began to devise a desperate plan, Heck said, "For now, we gotta let folks know what's happening, so they can decide what to do. Things are about to get downright exciting here."

"They will stand with you."

"We'll see. But it has to be their choice. A man who chooses to defend his home will always fight harder than a man paid to take it."

Hope felt sick to her stomach. She scooped up an oblivious Tor and held him close. This was their home, not Dumay's. Why did these people have to come here and do these horrible things? And why in the world would the army agree to help Dumay?

Ultimately, the answers to those questions didn't matter. All that mattered was what they did, how things turned out.

"This is going to be bad, isn't it?" she asked.

Heck nodded. "I won't lie. Some of us are going to die. Maybe even most of us. You and your mama and the Widow can round up the women and children and get them back in the cave. If something happens to us, you'll have plenty of food and water, and you'll be able to defend that narrow hallway pretty easily. We'll set up a barricade at one end for you."

Hope stared at him in disbelief. "Hector Martin, Jr., if you think—"

"It's the only way, Hope. I wish I could send you to Fort Bridger, but the miners are up by the trail. And they're probably still watching the way to Laramie, too. Once the soldiers arrive, they will take pity on you no matter how the rest of this shakes out. Orders or no orders, they will make sure you and the kids are safe. Now come on, Hope, quit looking at me that way. You know I'm right."

"I most certainly do not know you are right, Heck. If you think I'm going to leave you, there must be something wrong with your head. This is my home, too, and my fight. I will be on the walls of this fort with a rifle, and I'm sure those walls will be crowded. Most of the women will be just as eager to turn back Dumay's thugs. Let the elderly tend the children, though the older children will no doubt stay by our side, reloading rifles."

Heck started to say something, and she braced herself for an argument, but he closed his mouth, nodded, and chuckled then drew her and Tor into an embrace.

"My fierce wife, I never should have thought you'd wait in a cave. We'll be lucky to have you and the rest of the women's brigade. In the meantime, I'm working on a plan that I hope will avoid an all-out war."

Hope listened as Heck explained what he was going to do.

Even as he spelled out the details, however, Hope's angry, impatient mind worked out a plan of her own... one she couldn't share with Heck because he would never let her do it.

But that wouldn't stop Hope. Neither would the danger. She had always been able to summon courage when she needed it, and besides, she had always loved surprising her husband.

And this plan would certainly do that.

CHAPTER 38

O nce more, Dumay paced the floorboards of his cabin.
Leaning against the wall, Frank Wedge was making
less of an effort to conceal his impatience. "The men are restless. Some are breaking. Three more deserted this morning."

"How is that possible?" Dumay shouted. "Didn't I make it
clear? The punishment for desertion is death."

"Why don't you track down those three deserters and
remind them?"

"I can do without your sarcasm, Mr. Wedge."

"You need to pay attention to your men," Wedge said. "Half
of them are so jumpy, they just want to ride up there and kill
everyone. The other half are scared out of their minds. You
hear them out there saying this isn't what they signed up for."

"It's exactly what they signed up for!"

"We should kill Heck Martin," Wedge said, his pale blue eyes
glimmering like patches of ice over a winter stream. "Now,
before it's too late."

"Absolutely not," Dumay said and slapped a hand on the desk for emphasis. "You keep forgetting. The army is on its way. They will be here any day. Maybe even this afternoon. Then, we'll take the valley with no loss of men or reputation. All we have to do is wait."

"You're wrong," Wedge sat flatly, turning his back and opening the door.

"Where do you think you're going?"

"If you refuse to let me call out Heck Martin, I'd better go check the men and make sure they aren't deserting. Otherwise, you and I will be the only ones left."

"Fine," Dumay snapped, wanting to be rid of the tiresome killer for a moment. He was sick to death of Wedge's gloomy pessimism.

Wedge left and closed the door behind him, and for the next several minutes, Dumay paced back and forth, thinking things over.

He was so close now, so close to doing what he had come all this way, at great expense, to do: crush Heck Martin.

He was going to repay Martin for the humiliation he had suffered at the graveyard auction. The papers had caught wind of that humiliation, of course, and shouted the news not only in San Francisco, which was bad enough, but in the East as well, telling just enough of the story to make Dumay a laughingstock across the country.

Well, he was writing a new ending to that story now. He only hoped Heck Martin was captured alive, so he could spell out all these things and watch Martin's reaction.

That would be a truly delicious moment.

Meanwhile, as he paced, he allowed his thoughts to drift

deeper into the situation and consider the gold that must lay within Martin's cave.

He had not come here for the gold, hadn't even allowed himself to really think on it, since he was so focused on repaying Martin, but he suspected there was a lot of gold here, perhaps more, even, than he had ever discovered in California, and that was saying something.

No, he had not come here for the gold, but he did find it soothing to think of what he might gain here after the army arrived and cleaned up this mess for him.

A knock sounded at the door.

Dumay opened it. Seeing Jem Pulcher and the spy, Wyatt Henley, he ushered them inside.

"It occurs to me, Mr. Pulcher," Dumay said, "that I haven't seen your cousin, Mr. Boon, in quite some time. Where is he?"

Jem Pulcher smiled nastily. "He's been laying low."

"Has he deserted?"

"Trace? No. He's too scared to run. But he's too scared to show his face around here, too."

"He needn't be frightened. We're only cracking down on the traitors, those who try to abandon us."

"Trace ain't afraid of you," Pulcher said. "He's scared of Heck Martin. Figures Heck'll get the best of you and then deal with us for stabbing him in the back. His words, not mine. I'm with you to the bitter end, Mr. Dumay."

For some reason, the notion disturbed Dumay. Any end shared with Pulcher would be bitter, indeed.

He turned to Wyatt and asked the spy for a report.

"You'd better get ready, Mr. Dumay," Wyatt said. "Maguire ain't doing so hot."

"Maguire?"

"The cowboy your men beat up."

"Oh right, him. What about him?"

"He's on death's doorstep. Folks are upset about it. If he dies, they're gonna come for you, no two ways about it."

Dumay repressed a shudder. "Do you really think he's going to die?"

Wyatt shrugged. "He doesn't look so good."

Dumay scowled. "That's troubling news."

"Why?" Jem Pulcher said. "It's perfect."

"Perfect?" Dumay said, wheeling on the man. "The army will be here at any moment."

"Which is why you want Heck to come at you now," Pulcher said. "He's friends with some of them soldiers. Maybe even all of them. How hard are they really gonna push him?"

Dumay just looked at him, but inside, he reeled with dismay.

Was Pulcher speaking the truth?

Yes, he believed he was.

He had known that Heck Martin had a friend among the officers, but his letter had taken care of that. Why had no one told him that Martin also had friends among the soldiers?

Because no one he'd hired had known that, of course. Not the politicians or General Bradbury or the riders who'd carried the letter.

None of them would have known.

Only the soldiers at Fort Laramie would know that.

Suddenly, he reconsidered the seeming delay in the cavalry's arrival. Is that why they hadn't come sooner?

Were they dragging their feet, buying Heck time?

If so, time for what?

And what, precisely, would these soldiers, if they were indeed friends of Heck Martin, do when they arrived?

"Here's what I'm thinking," Pulcher said. "You want this Maguire to die. He's dies, everybody gets angry, and comes at you. So be it. We got enough men to take them. Especially if we fight here. Let them come at us. We'll cut them to ribbons. We still got more rifles than they do."

Not many more, Dumay thought, but Pulcher was making sense.

"And then, when the army arrives to find their buddy dead," Pulcher said, spreading his hands, "you just say hey, what was I supposed to do? He attacked us."

Dumay nodded. It was a brilliantly simple plan, the perfect partner to his original plan, which had hinged on Heck Martin doing enough for Dumay's letter to Colonel Harper to have some teeth.

"I see what you're saying," Dumay said. "But how—"

"Wyatt can finish Maguire off."

"Me?"

"Sure," Pulcher said. "Just go back and put a pillow over his face."

Wyatt shrugged. "I could do that, but I'm not going back again after in case somebody figures out I did it. If I do this, you gotta take me in."

Dumay waved his hand in a dismissive gesture. "That's fine, fine. Just go back and do it. Put a pillow over his face, make sure he's dead, and then come back and let me know."

"Might want to stick around long enough to put the idea in their head," Pulcher said to Wyatt. "You know, stir them up, tell them this is it, they gotta get Dumay."

Wyatt shook his head. "No way. If I do this, I'm running out before anybody finds him. Besides, they don't need any prodding. Trust me. I've been listening to them. This man is their friend. And over there, friendship means something. He dies, they'll come running."

Dumay nodded. "All right. That's it. Good. Yes, that is the plan. Go back and kill Maguire. In the meantime, I'll tell Mr. Wedge to—"

At that moment, without so much as a light rapping, the door swung wide, and a young woman of incredible beauty strode into the room, her green eyes flashing with anger.

CHAPTER 39

Hope had never been so terrified in all her life. But her courage did not fail her, and refusing to let her fear show, she strode straight into the room, her eyes locked on the man she recognized as Percival Dumay.

"Who are you?" Dumay demanded.

"I am Hope Martin, wife of Heck Martin."

Dumay was clearly flabbergasted. "How did you get past my guards?"

"I just asked politely, and they showed me the way. Which wasn't all that surprising. These men haven't seen a woman in a long time, after all."

That had been her biggest concern coming here. What if a group of brutal men tried to take advantage of her?

But she had gambled on the chivalry so often seen in frontier men, who tended to be a romantic, sentimental lot.

And despite the rough appearance of Dumay's thugs, they

had indeed acted like gentlemen and treated her with respect, praise God.

In return, she had smiled and voiced her gratitude and allowed one of the men to help her down from Dolly, explaining loudly enough for all to hear that she appreciated his help dismounting especially because she was with child.

Now, noticing Wyatt Henley standing there, Hope filled with fresh rage and skewered the treacherous snake with a sharp glare.

"So you're the one. Heck knew someone was betraying us. The day Dusty got hurt, you said men with guns ran you off, but now I see the truth. You were with them all along."

"It isn't what it looks like," Wyatt said.

"Oh? Really? What is it, then? Why are you here?"

"I'm just trying to be diplomatic."

Jem Pulcher laughed like he'd never witnessed anything so funny.

"And you," she said, pointing at Jem. "What a backstabbing scoundrel. After Heck saved you and showed you mercy, this is his thanks? You guide an army here to kill us?"

"No one is here to kill you, Mrs. Martin," Dumay said quickly. "I do not wish violence."

"Well, then, you had better get rid of these ungrateful rats before I claw their eyes out."

Clearly shocked by her choice of words, Dumay ordered the other three men from the room.

Wyatt hesitated in the doorway. "It really isn't what it looks like, ma'am. I'll explain everything."

Jem Pulcher laughed and slapped Wyatt on the shoulder. "Good luck with that, buddy. She ain't buying it."

Hope stared at Wyatt until he squirmed. "I suggest you leave the territory as quickly as you can, because I'm going to tell Heck everything. When he hears about your betrayal, he's going to come hunting you. And when he finds you, he's going to torture you to death—Indian style!"

Heck would never do such a thing, of course, but Wyatt didn't know that, and she enjoyed watching his eyes bulge. He hurried outside, closing the door behind him and Jem Pulcher.

"Now, Mrs. Martin," Dumay said in a civilized tone, and offered a smile as if they were sitting down to tea, "to what do I owe the honor of—oh!"

She pushed the .41 caliber Philadelphia Derringer into his face, letting him feel the cold steel barrel against the bridge of his nose.

"You come in here," Hope said, "threatening us, hurting us, paying off politicians, and push my husband—a good man, well-known and well-loved in these parts—trying to make him fight against your hired thugs and kill people he doesn't want to kill. Then try to sick the army on us. Do you really think we'll quit?"

"Mrs. Martin, I—"

"Do you? Do you think we'll quit? Because we don't quit, Dumay. Not Heck, not me, not any of us."

Her hand trembled—not with fear but with anger. She was surprised to realize that she wanted to pull the trigger. But of course, that would be a terrible mistake.

Her hand wasn't the only thing shaking. Dumay's lower lip trembled as if he were standing in a tub of ice water.

"Mrs. Martin, please lower your weapon, or I will be forced to call my men."

"I'm going to have my say. If you call them to stop me, I will put a bullet between your eyes."

"Then my men would execute you."

"Would they? Why? You'd already be dead and couldn't pay them anymore. Or are these men truly loyal to you? Would they kill a woman? A pregnant woman? One who had nothing but smiles and curtseys for them outside?"

She paused, letting her words sink in.

Dumay sputtered as the color drained from his face.

"Why would they do that?" she said. "To honor your memory? No. They work for money. They don't care about you. All I would have to say is that you tried to force yourself on me, and they would believe it. They won't even bury you. They'll let the wolves chew your bones."

Dumay looked horrified. "What manner of woman are you?"

"The manner of woman who loves her husband, her children, her home, and her neighbors. I need you to understand that, Mr. Dumay. And I need you to understand what will happen if you don't leave here immediately. Heck and I aren't alone. You might outnumber us, but this valley is full of people ready to fight to the death. If it comes to war, we will all be hunting you. Not your men. *You.*"

She poked his forehead with the barrel, eliciting another gasp, then backed away, opened the door, and left the cabin.

When she had gone, Dumay collapsed to the dirt floor, his whole body convulsing with the aftershocks of terror.

A moment later, Wedge came through the door and towered over him, peering down at Dumay as if he were a bug stuck on its back, its tiny legs scratching impotently at the air.

"That woman," Dumay gasped. "Came in here, threatened me. Shoot her!"

Wedge continued to look at him for a moment. "No, sir. That I will not do. Now, though, maybe you'll finally let me do what I *will* do."

CHAPTER 40

While folks back at the fort prepared for the worst, Heck and a dozen good men rode down the valley.

They didn't even bother sneaking in from the ridge. They merely rode down the line and around the bend, surprising Dumay's cattle guards, who likely never expected such a bold advance.

Dumay had apparently expected something, however, because he had ten men standing there.

"Hands in the air, or we open fire," Heck said. "You fight, you die."

One of them foolishly shouldered his rifle.

Heck's Sharps rifle boomed loudly, and the man went down hard, never to rise again.

The other nine guards dropped their weapons and raised their hands.

Which was understandable, and not just because of what

had happened to their friend. They were surrounded by Heck's riders, who spread out, rifles at the ready.

"Now, that's just a shame," Heck said. "Why did he do that? I told him what would happen, didn't I? You all heard me. Shucks. I told him if he tried to fight, I'd kill him. Well, now I'm fixing to tell the rest of you what's gonna happen if you keep hanging around here. As you see, my men and me, we're no strangers to death. We will fight to the last man. This is our home. We fought bandits, Indians, and traitors, and killed them all—just like we'll kill you if you stick around."

The men stared at him in horror.

"You know," Heck said conversationally, "I was just gonna let you folks sit here, watch you starve, then let winter freeze the rest of you. But your boss, Dumay, he must not care a lick about you, because he called in the army, and that means I gotta finish this now."

"Don't kill us," one of the men pleaded.

"Oh, I won't kill you. Not yet. Only if you stay and fight. Now, take out any other weapons and set them on the ground. Nice and easy. You know what happens to folks who resist."

Dumay's men timidly surrendered their weapons.

Shorty, who had already captured the guards' only horse, said, "Should we take their boots, too, Heck?"

"Nah, these men will need boots to walk back to California. But we will take their cattle."

"You can't take the cows," one of the men said. "We'll starve."

"Should've considered that before you shot and stampeded my cattle up on the trail."

"That wasn't us, it was Dumay."

"Well, that's a shame. You boys threw in with the worst sort of man. You'd best unhitch your wagons from his before it's too late. You stick with him, you're gonna die in this place. Just like this boy here."

He gestured with his barrel toward the dead man, who had been kind enough to die on his back, staring up at his former colleagues with a look of anguish locked on his ugly face.

"And just in case you think you boys might wipe us out and take our cattle and everything'll be okay, guess again. I've already sent word to a friend of mine at Fort Laramie, Major Avery Scottsdale, head of supply, that in the event of my death, all my cattle and supplies—a complete inventory of which, right down to the last cracker, I included with my letter—become the property of the U.S. Army. Major Scottsdale might not be able to stop Dumay's cowardly, criminal activity here, but he will see to it that my will is honored and that his men take every head of cattle, every crumb of food, and every stick of firewood back to Fort Laramie. I saved his life once, and he won't forget that. He will despise you, and he will do everything in his power to make sure you all die."

The men stared, putting it all together in their reeling minds.

"In other words," Heck continued, "you will starve. I know Dumay is paying you boys well, but you can't eat gold. Though I suppose if you stick around for winter, you'll get hungry enough to try. You've got just enough time to beat winter if you leave now. After the first snow falls, though, it's over. Blizzards in this territory are like nothing you've ever seen. Men go out, meaning to walk to an outbuilding, lose their way in the wall of white. Next day, their family finds them frozen to death, ten feet from the door. Get out now before it's too late. The Indians are already watching you, of course. They smell your weakness."

"Speak of the devil, Heck," Shorty said, and pointed to the ridge. "Look, there's one now."

Looking up, they saw a man with a feather headdress sitting high above and muttered with fear.

One of Dumay's men squinted. "He don't look like an Injun to me. Awful pale in the face, ain't he?"

"That's just the sunlight is all," another said.

"No," the doubting man said. "Speaking of sun, look at the light flash from his eyes. I think he's wearing spectacles."

Heck felt a stab of concern. The whole plan hinged on these men believing they faced overwhelming obstacles. Why hadn't Doc taken his glasses off before riding up there?

But then one of them pointed and said, "There's another."

"And another."

"There's a whole bunch."

Which confused Heck greatly. He only had one feathered headdress, a gift from the Horse Creek Treaty, and only one person, Doc, pretending to be an Indian.

Then he had to suppress his laughter as a stream of Shoshones rode into view high up on the ridge and sat their horses beside Doc, staring down like so many hanging judges.

His brave, dark-haired, little brother glared down from the very center of the group, which grew and grew and grew.

"You go back," Heck told the men. "Tell your friends this is it. Your last chance. And take your buddy with you." He gestured again toward the dead man. "He'll tell them, too, in ways they won't be able to ignore."

CHAPTER 41

On the ride back, Hope felt exhilarated to have delivered such a strong message on her own.

It had gone perfectly, praise God. Dumay's men had even gathered around, several of them wanting to help her onto Dolly.

She'd let them, of course. It wasn't that she'd needed the help. She just understood men and knew that if she let them help her, they would be more likely to help her again if Dumay came running out and demanded they harm her.

Now, having put hundreds of yards between herself and the camp, she relaxed, savoring the moment as she followed the trail, drawing close to the edge of the wooded slope at the western edge of the field.

She thought of Dumay and Wyatt Henley. How frightened they had been.

Wyatt was probably halfway to California already because he knew how deadly Heck was.

But what about Dumay?

Yes, she had frightened him, but how would he respond when there wasn't a gun in his face? Dumay was out of his element here, but he remained a strong and powerful man used to achieving his goals.

Would her message unnerve him, as she had hoped, or push him over the edge and—

Wyatt rode out of the trees and blocked her path, pointing a rifle at her.

Hope gasped.

"I knew you'd come back this way. Saw your tracks and followed them here, where it's nice and private." Grinning, Wyatt brought his horse close to hers. She didn't think of him as a fighter, but at this range, no one could miss.

"You shouldn't have told me your plans, Mrs. Martin," Wyatt said. "Now, I can't let you return home. You can either come with me and be my woman, or I can shoot you dead right here and go on my own."

"You don't want to shoot me. Then you wouldn't have a hostage," Hope said, forcing a smile onto her face, then looked over his shoulder and nodded in a trick she had played on childhood friends countless times back in Kentucky, being a girl who always loved a good joke. "Look, here comes Heck now."

Under normal circumstances, Wyatt might not have fallen for it, but terrified as he was, he spun at the mention of Heck, the source of his terror.

When his barrel swung away, Hope lifted her own pistol, drew back the hammer, and pulled the trigger, just as Heck had shown her time and time again over the years.

The bullet hit Wyatt as he was turning back around, striking him higher than she had intended, not in the chest, as Heck had taught her, but in the throat.

His horse reared, and Wyatt tumbled off, dead before he struck the ground.

Dolly shook her head and stomped her feet.

For a second, Hope was too shocked to even calm her horse. Then she leaned to one side and vomited, shaking all over, asking God for forgiveness and telling herself that she had only done what she had to do in self-defense.

When she was steady enough to ride again, she navigated Dolly around the dead body and headed for home, taking the time to catch the reins of Wyatt's horse.

But she could not bring herself to fetch the dead man's rifle or search his pockets. She wanted nothing from him, wanted only to get away and get home to her family.

Riding out into the open, where Dumay's valley met her own, she was thrilled to see Heck and some of the men from Hope City astride horses, driving Dumay's cattle northward.

Several of Dumay's men were running southeast across the field and away from Heck, awkwardly lugging another man, who was either dead or badly injured, in the direction of their camp.

Heck spotted her and sat up very straight in his saddle.

She waved, laughing.

Recognizing her, Heck looked confused, but he lifted his hat and waved back, filling her heart with joy until she saw riders north of his position, coming down the trail from the direction of Hope City, two dozen men racing toward her beloved.

"Heck!" she cried. "Look out! It's the cavalry!"

CHAPTER 42

D umay flinched at the distant gunshot.

"It's time," Wedge said. "You've already waited too long. Everything is coming together now. Killing time is here."

Dumay shook his head, rocked to the core. "It wasn't supposed to end this way. I planned everything. Paid all the right people. Everything was set. All we had to do was push them a little, then wait for the army."

"We can't wait another minute for the army. Heck Martin is coming. You let his people get into a killing frenzy, you will lose everything."

Dumay shook his head. "We outnumber them three to one."

"Not anymore. And a third of your men are up the trail with the mining wagons."

Dumay's eyes bulged at that. "But we still have all these soldiers. We—"

"These men aren't soldiers. They're miners with rifles. There's a difference. They lack the discipline to stand. And like

I've been trying to tell you, they've been breaking ranks and deserting every day. When was the last time you took a head count?"

"But we warned them. We told them. You showed them. The punishment for desertion is—"

"Too little, too late," Wedge said. "Nothing could stop them from running now. I thought maybe it would help, but it didn't."

A coughing fit seized Dumay. This wasn't possible. Just wasn't possible. "But I paid them well."

"And they want to live long enough to spend that money. Now, let me go and—"

"Mr. Dumay," Trace Boon yodeled, stumbling into the room, pale with fright. "Heck Martin and his men are at the edge of the valley, sir. Someone's down. One of our men. Boys think it might be Chip Timmerman. They say he's dead, sir."

"Muster the men," Dumay commanded to no one in particular. "We're going to ride out there and drive these people back. Gather everyone. I want to show our full force."

"Well, sir," Trace said, "a lot of men seem to be... leaving, sir."

"Leaving?"

"Yes, sir. Don't be mad at me, sir. I'm still here, ain't I? But yeah, a bunch of fellas are hightailing it south."

"They can't leave. I paid them for the duration!"

Trace Boon just stared at him, his mouth slightly ajar, looking terribly stupid.

How did I ever get myself involved with these people? Dumay wondered incredulously.

Wedge spread his hands, a placid expression on his face.

"Well," Dumay told Boon, "you go get them before they

leave. Tell them we need them now." His mind scrambled, chewing at the situation like a rat trying to gnaw its way out of an iron box. "Tell them I'll give an extra hundred dollars to everyone who stands with me today!"

Trace Boon frowned. "I'll do my best, sir."

As Boon ducked out the door, a nervous-looking man whose name Dumay could not remember stepped halfway inside the cabin, his hat clutched to his belly.

"Sir," the frightened man reported, "there's a bunch of Indians up on the ridge."

"Indians?" Dumay blurted.

This didn't even seem possible. It was as if God Himself was conspiring against him now.

Though, of course, Dumay had never believed in the Almighty. He had earned his fortune through talent and effort and a little luck from time to time. He had done it himself and wasn't about to give credit to some mythical power above.

"Yes, sir. A whole bunch of them."

"Define a bunch," Wedge said.

"I don't know, sir. I seen a whole line of 'em up there and more a comin'. Forty? Fifty? I don't know. I didn't hang around to count, neither. Figured you'd want to know as soon as possible."

"What are they doing?" Dumay demanded, hating the panic in his own voice.

"They was waiting, sir."

"Waiting?"

"Yes, sir."

"Waiting for what?"

"Waiting for Heck Martin, sir. They was just staring down at him, and he held up a hand, like he was saying for them to wait, and they just set there, I guess waiting for him to tell them what to do next."

"That's preposterous," Dumay said, half-believing it. "How could Martin control an army of savages?"

"Heck Martin is well known in these parts," Wedge commented calmly. "Respected. Liked, even. He's probably traded with these Indians. And don't forget. When the army put together that big treaty last year, Heck had a hand in it. I'd say you're in real trouble now."

Dumay was flabbergasted. "What... should I do?"

"Mr. Dumay," Wedge said, "you have tried your best. But now it's time for me to do things my way. Otherwise, you're fixing to lose everything you have. And I mean everything."

"Yes," Dumay said, nodding vehemently as if by doing so he could really believe the sentiment. How had it come to this? And how was he going to restore his reputation after making this decision? "Yes, that's it. Do it your way. Kill Heck Martin. Kill him and make these others go away."

"I don't know if that's possible anymore," Wedge said. "Getting the others to go, I mean. This should've been done a long time ago, like I said. But it's our only hope."

Dumay nodded again, realizing now that the killer had been right all along. Why hadn't Dumay listened to him?

The answer was simple. He hadn't listened because he'd been so determined to ruin Martin and rub his face in it, so concerned with keeping his reputation intact...

"Meanwhile," Wedge said, "you get someplace safe and wait for me to come back."

"I'll stay right here."

Wedge shook his head. "This is the first place they'll look for you. Get up in the woods southeast of here and keep an eye. If I don't come back, hightail it to San Francisco. Don't come back for anything, don't look for help, and don't expect mercy. Just go as fast as your horse can carry you."

Dumay was aghast. Just this morning, he wouldn't have thought this turn of events even possible. "Alone?"

"Yes, if you value your life. These men feel no loyalty to you. They wouldn't hesitate to kill you for your gold—or just to pay you back for getting them into this mess. Go now. Get into the woods, and if I don't return, head west and don't stop till you hit the Pacific."

They were interrupted by yet another messenger. "Sir, more riders are coming down the trail toward Heck."

Dumay felt a thrill. "The army?"

"I don't know, sir. I just saw a bunch of riders is all."

Dumay clenched his fists. Here it was! Victory! The army had arrived. Once again, he had saved himself through planning, political connections, and paying off the right people.

He never should have doubted himself. He never should have let his faith in himself be shaken!

"In case it's not the army, you'd best do like I say and get into the woods," Wedge said. "I'll take the men we have left and ride out to meet Heck."

"Okay, Mr. Wedge."

"We can't afford a large-scale engagement. Even if the cavalry is here—and my gut tells me that's not the army out there—we would need a big detachment to turn the tables back in our favor. But our goose isn't cooked just yet. I'm still planning to turn things back our way by calling out Heck Martin, man to man, and killing him in a fair fight."

And then Wedge smiled with such cool confidence that Dumay wondered how he had ever doubted the man. This was not San Francisco. This was the wilderness. And in the wilderness, men like Wedge—and, though Dumay hated to admit it, Heck Martin—held the only power that really mattered.

"Be careful," he said absurdly—but what else could he say in a moment like this?

Wedge chuckled. "Don't worry, boss. This is why you hired me. I'm good at this. Very, very good."

CHAPTER 43

Heck turned, fearing the worst. Then, seeing the approaching riders, he laughed aloud.

He was so surprised to see the men riding his way—especially the gray-bearded old coot at the front—that for the moment, he even forgot the question burning in his mind: *what had Hope been doing south of here?*

"Heck Martin," the old mountain man crowed. "Heard you got yourself in a bind and figured I'd best come over and save your hide yet again."

"Rabbit Foot!" Heck shouted with delight, riding over to meet the men.

Behind his dear old friend was a motley crew of frontiersmen he mostly recognized. Amos Johnson, Skeeter Tate, Rides with Wolves, and several others he knew to be hunters and scouts from Fort Laramie.

Heck clasped hands with the friend he'd missed dearly over recent years. "Rabbit Foot. It's good to see you."

"Good to see you, too, boy. I never thought I'd say this, but you've grown. Look at you. Like a grizzly bear in Buckskins. Are we too late? Did we miss the fight?"

"No, you're just in time," Heck said. "And so are those friends."

He nodded toward where Seeker, Black Cloud, and what looked like a hundred Shoshone warriors were now descending the long slope.

Rabbit Foot cackled wildly. "Them boys is with us? You always was a showoff, Heck!"

Heck praised God for His grace and mercy and favor. He praised Him for these friends and for delivering them in Heck's moment of great need. It was humbling, and he felt a lump in his throat, temporarily weakened by overwhelming gratitude.

"Here come the miners," A.J. Plum said.

Heck's men spread out, rifles at the ready.

There were only a couple of dozen miners. Where were the others?

Heck quickly scanned his surroundings, watching for movement or the flash of sunlight upon metal, but he saw no one trying to flank him.

Had that many deserted?

Whatever the case, he saw no sign of Dumay himself.

He did, however, see Dumay's hired killer, Frank Wedge, who rode at the front of the men, carrying a white flag.

"Hold your fire," Heck called to his men, honoring the flag.

Wedge and the others stopped a hundred yards away.

"I'm gonna ride out and see what they want," Heck said.

"Careful," Rabbit Foot said. "Could be a trap."

"Yeah, well, if it is, shoot him for me."

"Guaranteed," Rabbit Foot said, and patted his trusty Hawken.

Heck rode up to the enemy line. A few of Dumay's men looked grimly determined. Most looked lost and nervous.

These men, Heck realized, had not stayed out of loyalty to Dumay or any willingness to fight. They had stayed because they were scared to desert.

Wedge merely nodded, his face as calm and relaxed as if he and Heck were two neighbors fixing to chat about nice weather.

Only they weren't. Each meant to kill the other.

Heck understood that. And he supposed he had known it would come down to this from the first moment he'd seen Wedge, even before someone had identified him.

Because some men were killers. He had seen that in Wedge upon their first meeting, and he read it in the man's relaxed confidence now.

"White flag, huh?" Heck said.

"That's for the others," Wedge said. "Not us."

"I figured. Where's Dumay?"

"Someplace safe."

"There is no place safe in the wilderness."

"You understand why I'm here."

"To face me."

"That's right."

Heck tilted his head, thinking. "Why?"

"That's what I told Dumay I'd do."

"But everything's changed. We have you now."

Wedge shook his head. "You have *them*. Nobody has me. Dumay's hoping when I kill you, your friends will break off."

Heck laughed. "Not a chance. My friends and me, we stick together. I die, they'll still set things right."

Wedge nodded. "I see that now. It doesn't matter. The real reason I have to face you, well—it isn't pride, exactly—but I have to see."

"See what?"

"If you're as good as they say."

"I'll save you the trouble," Heck said, not wanting to kill this man. He had nothing against Wedge. Killing him would be a waste, nothing more. "I am as good as they say. Now, why don't you just surrender your guns and ride west so nobody else needs to die."

Wedge smiled and shook his head slowly. "Can't. Wouldn't be worth a half-penny if I turned tail now."

Heck nodded. "I understand. How are we going to do this?"

They worked it out and called witnesses forward from both sides, shook hands, then paced out the distance and stood, facing one another, with thirty yards of well-grazed pasture-land between them.

"You boys go ahead and get your shooting irons into position," Rabbit Foot said.

Heck pulled the big Colt Walker from his belt, straightened his long arm against his body, and cocked the hammer.

The old iciness settled over him, chilling the world, slowing it, and leaving him calm yet ready.

Wedge would be fast and accurate. Heck couldn't just stand there, trading lead, or they would both die.

He shifted his weight to the right, ready to fight.

"Draw!" Rabbit Foot shouted.

Wedge flung his free hand out to the side as he lifted the

pistol, meaning to aim down its barrel, but Heck merely tilted his own barrel and fired from the thigh, a thing he'd done many times in the past.

Wedge jerked, struck by the round Heck had snapped from down low. The killer's muzzle stabbed flame, his aim knocked askew.

Heck sprang off his right foot, lurching to the left, away from the natural sweep of Wedge's weapon, drew back the hammer, and fired again.

A miss.

Wedge swung his arm back in Heck's direction, and both men fired at the same time—once, twice, three times—in a steady roll of thunder and lightning that had no place in this sunny meadow.

Heck moved with each shot, not wanting to be a stationary target and did his best to fire accurately through the cloud of acrid gun smoke.

He knew he'd been hit more than once, but his body still worked, so he kept fighting, dropping to one knee beneath the smoke and firing his last cylinder even as Wedge's pistol barked again.

Heck's hat fell from his head as a line of fire burned across his scalp.

Wedge, his white shirt now stained red, dropped to the ground.

Heck raced forward, meaning to finish this at close quarters, which would be faster than trying to reload, but reaching the gunman, he saw that he needn't have hurried.

Wedge was dead.

Praise God, the war was over.

CHAPTER 44

"So they just left?" Captain Coney asked.

"Yes, sir," Heck said. He sat at the head of the table with Tor in his lap, feeding the boy little pieces of beef that Hope had cut up.

"Would you care for more potatoes, officers?" Hope asked.

Captain Coney gratefully accepted, as did his lieutenant. Neither of the men, of course, had any idea that their smiling hostess had killed a man during the final conflict.

As it turned out, Wyatt Henley was one of only a few men who died in the war for Heck's Valley.

Upon Wedge's death, Dumay's forces surrendered their arms, which made sense, considering they faced Heck and all his friends, including a hundred Shoshone warriors.

Heck, wounded only superficially in his fight with Wedge, drove the miners off, allowing them to take two wagons loaded with provisions, along with half a dozen of Dumay's cows to help them survive the journey West.

The rest of Dumay's things, including the remaining cattle, wagons, horses, and mining equipment, Heck claimed as the spoils of war, though much of this, along with additional cattle from his own herd, he gave to friends who had come to help him.

Heck thanked God for those friends. Without them, things might have turned out very differently, and both sides would have suffered catastrophic losses.

As we move through life, we must always bear its burdens as best we can, but it's good to remember one's friends and help as we're able. Doing so is a reward unto itself and because we are loving our neighbors, we are doing nothing less than the will of God.

Beyond that, however, by helping others, we up the chances that when we someday find ourselves outgunned, our friends will come running, ready to kill or die on our behalf.

Heck's friends had done just that.

Dumay, on the other hand, had no friends. He had only henchmen and hangers on.

While Heck was settling things with Wedge, Dumay had headed off into the wilderness with the two rats who'd started all this trouble: Jem Pulcher and Trace Boon.

Black Cloud offered to track them down, but Heck waved him off.

"Let them go, my friend," he'd said.

Heck had no idea how, exactly, the trio expected to make it all the way back to California, but he assumed Dumay carried a good deal of gold and further assumed Jem and Trace knew that.

Dumay had better sleep with one eye open, Heck figured, because those boys were not his friends.

Whatever happened to them along the way, no matter how terrible, they'd earned it. And more.

A few days later, the soldiers had arrived, having obviously made no great haste. Just as obviously, they were relieved to find the situation had resolved itself. None of them had wanted to face Heck and whatever force he had cobbled together, especially because none of them believed in their mission in the first place.

"Well," Captain Coney said, enjoying his beef and potatoes, "it will be my pleasure to report to Colonel Harper that Mr. Dumay had a change of heart and abandoned his property here."

The question of Dumay's property lingered in Heck's mind. Once things had settled down, he would compose a letter to Able Dean and do his best to secure not only his land but the surrounding country as well.

He had already let his herd back into the grassy valleys below his, and Dumay's structures there now served as bunkhouses for the men who tended the cattle. They jokingly called the cluster of cabins Cowtown. The name caught on, and Heck reckoned it might stick.

Hopefully, he could buy Cowtown and the surrounding valleys, since he now understood he needed the grass, and clear up any confusion concerning his own title.

He didn't know how much ground Dumay had purchased here in the wilderness, but whatever the case, he was determined to buy land surrounding it. By purchasing the open notch to the southwest and a portion of canyon further downstream, he could block every approach to the southern valleys and lock away all that lovely grass and water.

He should have thought of this before, of course, but that's the way life is. Sometimes, you can't see the totality of a situation until that situation punches you in the mouth.

Well, this problem with Dumay had certainly sucker punched Heck, but he'd weathered the storm, praise God, and now he was going to do what he could do to fix his earlier mistakes and keep something like this from happening again.

But first, he would enjoy the spoils of war. Not the mining equipment, which he was in no hurry to employ, but time with his family—because that is the greatest treasure of all.

That night, lying in bed, Heck sensed Hope staring up at him. He laid down the book he was reading and smiled at his pretty wife. "Want me to put out the candle? Is it keeping you awake?"

"Don't put it out, Heck. I was just looking at you is all. I'm very thankful... for everything."

"So am I," he said, and leaned down to kiss her. "I still can't believe what you did, riding down to Dumay's camp like that. It was a reckless thing to do."

"We've already talked about that, and like I said, if I went back to the beginning, I'd do it over again."

"Even knowing what ended up happening with Wyatt?"

"Everything. It was terrible, but I did what I had to do, and I've made my peace with God. Besides, you yourself said my visit must've rattled Dumay."

"I'm sure it did."

"I needed him to know that this wasn't just about him and you. The rest of us were with you to the end, no matter what."

"Well, I appreciate that."

"You were pretty upset that I rode down there."

"I was. That's because I love you, and I hate to think of you taking such a risk." He smiled. "But you've always had a knack for surprising me, Hope, and you sure surprised me, doing what you did."

She laughed prettily. "I will never bore you, Heck Martin."

"No, ma'am, you surely won't. And I would never want a wife who walked behind me. I want my wife to walk right by my side—which is exactly what you do."

They kissed again, then Hope's expression grew more serious. "You are my man, Heck. Yonder lies our son, and he is my heart." She laid a hand on her belly. "Our second child is growing within me. This is our home, our valley, and our family and friends live just outside. This is our life, and God willing, we will destroy anyone who tries to take it from us."

CHAPTER 45

Weeks later, a ragged, emaciated figure stumbled out of the woods a hundred miles west of Heck's Valley.

He limped, breathing hoarsely, a torn and bloody wraith of a man wearing only one shoe. Like a frightened beast, he looked constantly in all directions, his eyes burning with fear and fever.

Torn by briars, splashed with mud, and swollen with mosquito bites, he lurched choppily forward and let out a strangled cry when he spotted the trail. Within the trail's deep ruts, water now sparkled with ice.

Percival Dumay's chuckle was as ragged as his clothing, the pockets of which still bulged and jangled, ironically enough, with a great number of golden coins, the entirety of which he would gladly trade for dry shoes and a hot meal.

He'd lost the coins for a while shortly after fleeing the disaster in the valley, when Pulcher and Boon had shown their true colors and turned on him, demanding his money as an advance against a future payment, they said, for returning him to San Francisco alive.

A lot of good the gold had done them.

Boon had died a fearful death when a huge, brown bear appeared seemingly out of thin air, knocked him to the ground, and proceeded to eat him alive. Dumay and Pulcher abandoned him and ran for their lives as Boon cried for help.

Pulcher lasted another week before stepping into a nest of sluggish rattlers all bundled together for warmth. Several sunk their fangs into his flesh, and that night, their poison transformed the odious Jem Pulcher into a grinning corpse distorted by the swelling.

Dumay had recaptured his gold and struggled on alone. He'd nearly frozen atop the mountains, hurt his hip sliding down the reverse slope, then stumbled in circles through a gloomy wood before splashing into the nightmarish swamp where he lost his shoe and, for a time, his mind.

He was injured, sick, and starving, but he had found the trail again, and this knowledge filled him with the first real hope he'd felt in days or perhaps even weeks.

Now, he could believe in his plan again. He would survive. He would return to San Francisco. And he would spend the rest of his life, if necessary, along with the rest of his massive fortune, to destroy Heck Martin and his cursed valley.

He didn't even want the gold anymore. He just wanted to kill Heck, his crazy wife, and all their friends and family. The cattle, too, would be exterminated, and the valley would be burned. The grass, the trees, the game… all of it.

He wouldn't be satisfied until Heck's Valley was a blackened scar upon the world. And then, perhaps, he would hire hundreds of wagons to salt that wretched earth.

These thoughts looped through his mind again and again as he limped doggedly over the trail.

Yes, he would have his revenge, and then they would see what good all of Heck Martin's precious friends would do him.

Finally, as the shadows were growing longer, Dumay spotted a weather-beaten sign and burst into laughter.

Fort Bridger, 2 Miles

"I made it," Dumay laughed. "I really made it!"

He staggered down the path and around the bend and lurched to a stop, almost crashing into a big Indian dressed like a white man.

"Friend," Dumay blurted, gnashing his teeth in a desperate smile.

The Indian looked back at him with no expression on his face.

"I'll give you money," Dumay said. "How much to take me to Fort Bridger?"

The Indian held up two thick fingers. "Two bits."

Dumay burst into laughter again. "Excellent. Wonderful. You have a deal, my good sir." He held out his hand.

The Indian just looked at it. "Two bits."

"Oh, right. Well, you shall have more than two bits," Dumay said, digging in his pocket and bringing out a twenty-dollar double eagle. "What do you say about that, eh? Two bits times eighty!"

The Indian shrugged his big shoulders, pocketed the coin, and started downhill toward Fort Bridger.

Dumay could have made it on his own, of course. The path

was clearly marked, and the trading post was only a short distance away now. But by hiring the big Indian, he had eliminated the chance of getting robbed instead.

Pleased with his cleverness, excited to at last be within easy reach of a post where he might rest and eat and clothe himself then find passage aboard a wagon the rest of the way to California, Dumay was feeling nothing short of bubbly.

"What is your name, good sir?" he asked the huge savage. He didn't really care about his name, of course. He was just so excited that he felt like talking.

"Two Bits."

"Two Bits?" Dumay laughed again. The stupid creature apparently only knew two words in the whole English language.

Once Martin was dead, Dumay decided, he would start offering top bounties for Indian scalps. It was a cause he believed in. The sooner these animals were exterminated the better.

Then the Indian surprised him, speaking something approaching a complete sentence in broken yet completely understandable English. "Do any job, two bits."

"Is that right? Well, I'll pay you ten of these shiny golden coins if you do something for me."

The Indian stopped walking and stared at him, waiting.

"I want you to kill someone," Dumay said, and involuntarily tittered at the notion.

The Indian shrugged again, clearly undaunted by the request. "Who?"

"A man not terribly far from here," Dumay said, and suddenly, he was trembling with excitement. Could it really be this simple? "He thinks he bested me, but no one bests Percival Dumay. I won't rest until he's dead. His name is Heck Martin."

The Indian stared at him with no expression on his stony face. His big hands lashed out and grabbed Dumay by the chin and the wild tangle of hair at the back of his head.

Trapped in the powerful man's grip, Dumay reeled with terror and confusion. "What is the meaning of this?"

"Heck friend," Two Bits said matter-of-factly, and twisted sharply, snapping Dumay's neck and killing him instantly.

Two Bits nodded with appreciation when he discovered and pocketed all the gold the man had been carrying. Then he tumbled the raggedy corpse into a deep ravine and promptly forgot about Dumay, turning his thoughts instead to the good things he might buy with these many coins.

CHAPTER 46

Heck and Seeker rode past the prospectors' graveyard to
the edge of the ridge, where they drew up their horses
at the sight of a toppled sign.

They dismounted and walked over and examined the
ground.

"Doesn't look like prospectors pulled it," Seeker said.

"Nope. It was the wind or maybe this big branch here that
knocked it down. Whatever the case, this sign fell to the passing
of time."

They stood there looking at it for a second. As always, a
brisk wind was blowing off the higher ground. Scented with
that strange sharpness Heck had always loved in this land, the
wind was colder today.

Seeker must've felt it, too. "Winter's coming."

Heck nodded. "It is."

From down in the valley, faintly, came the frantic knocking
of many hammers.

Over recent weeks, a good number of people had come into the valley, wanting to sink roots and expand Hope City.

Heck had accepted most proposals and asked only a few, like the surly bunch of riders yesterday, to keep on heading down the trail.

The newest settlers had arrived very late in the season, but the citizens of Hope City, many of whom knew what it was to be alone and desperate here in this wild place, lent a hand, raising cabins and barns, shops and corrals with surprising speed.

One of those swinging a hammer, Heck was pleased to know, was Dusty Maguire. Blind in one eye and stuck with a limp, Dusty worked for only short spurts before needing to rest, much as Heck had after his fight with the grizzly and Dave Chapman.

But Doc said Dusty would recover well, if not completely, and would be able to ride a horse again.

Dusty, always a cowboy, said that was good enough for him.

Seeker spoke then, and again, as was so often the case, his thoughts dovetailed into Heck's. "Sure is something, how fast things are building up down there. It boggles the mind."

"That it does."

"You reckon it's a mistake?"

"What's that, letting them stick around?"

"Letting things get built up, I mean. Letting the town get so big."

Heck paused for a second, surveying his mind for any fresh thoughts, but found none. Which made sense. He'd been over this time and time again, both in his own mind and talking with others, chief among them his wife, who thought it was a good thing.

"I reckon it's mostly for the best," he said.

"Mostly?"

"Yeah, mostly."

"Because people bring problems."

"People bring a lot of stuff. They bring skills and energy, babies and laughter, security in numbers, ideas..."

"And trouble."

"You are correct, little brother. People bring trouble."

Seeker nodded. "Town this big, there's bound to be trouble."

"Yup."

"What are we gonna do about it?"

"What we always do. We'll handle the bad stuff then get back to enjoying the good stuff."

"Sounds like a plan, big brother," Seeker said, kneeling and picking up the sign reading, *Heck's Valley. Private property. 24 square miles. Visitors are welcome. Trespassers are not. No prospecting, no panning. Owners: Seeker Yates, Hope Martin, Heck Martin.*

Heck glanced out once more across the valley, thankful that his gamble had paid off in the end.

Then Seeker held the stake straight, and Heck hammered their claim deep into this land he loved so very, very much.

#

THANK YOU FOR READING *HECK'S GAMBLE.*

Heck and Hope's adventures continue in *Heck'sStand.*

If you enjoyed this story, please be a friend and leave a review. When you leave even a short review, you just bought my family dinner, because Amazon will show the book to more people. I sure would appreciate your help.

If you enjoyed the book but don't have time to review, please consider leaving a 5-star rating. It's quick and simple and helps me get this new series off the ground.

I love Westerns and hope to bring you 8 or 10 a year. To hear about new releases, special sales, and giveaways, join my reader list.

Once more, thanks for reading. I hope our paths cross again.

Until then, don't approach a bull from the front, a horse from the rear, or a fool from any direction.

John

ABOUT THE AUTHOR

I was born six months before man landed on the moon and lucky enough to grow up in the country, where my family lived largely off the land.

When I wasn't fishing, exploring the woods, or weeding the garden, I devoured comic books like *Two-Gun Kid* and *The Rawhide Kid* before moving on to the exciting adventure stories of Jack London and Louis L'Amour.

Our black-and-white TV only got three channels, though you could lose one and pick up another if you went outside and messed with the antenna. On its grainy screen, we watched *Gunsmoke*, *Bonanza*, and movies starring John Wayne and Clint Eastwood.

Now a husband and father, I love traveling the West and reading history and fiction alike. My favorite authors are Louis L'Amour, Elmore Leonard, C.J. Petit, and R.O. Lane.

As a writer, I hope to entertain you with fun stories of the old West. My good guys are good, my bad guys are bad, and you'll always find a touch of romance to sweeten the grit.

If you'd like to keep in touch, join my newsletter HERE.

Printed in Great Britain
by Amazon

23806269R00148